T0068187

DARK MERCY

DARK MERCY

DAVE HART

DARK MERCY

iUniverse books may be ordered through booksellers or by contacting:

iUniverse
1663 Liberty Drive
Bloomington, IN 47403
www.iuniverse.com
844-349-9409

Because of the dynamic nature of the Internet, any web addresses or links contained in this book may have changed since publication and may no longer be valid. The views expressed in this work are solely those of the author and do not necessarily reflect the views of the publisher, and the publisher hereby disclaims any responsibility for them.

Any people depicted in stock imagery provided by Getty Images are models, and such images are being used for illustrative purposes only. Certain stock imagery © Getty Images.

ISBN: 978-1-6632-5892-2 (sc)
ISBN: 978-1-6632-5893-9 (e)

Library of Congress Control Number: 2023923928

Print information available on the last page.

iUniverse rev. date: 12/21/2023

Also available from the Author...

McKenzie 'Mac' Cole series

All That Remains by Dave Hart © 2022 iUniverse Publishing, Inc.

Tipping Point by Dave Hart © 2021 iUniverse Publishing, Inc.

All the Pretty Pieces by Dave Hart ©2020 iUniverse Publishing, Inc.

Adventures Along the Jersey Shore by Dave Hart & John Calu Copyright © 2015 Plexus Publishing, Inc.

- *The Treasure of Tucker's Island*
- *Mystery of the Jersey Devil*
- *Secret of the Painted Rock*
- *Lost Mission of Captain Carranza*
- *Riddle in the Sand*
- *Spirits of Cedar Bridge*
- *Storm Warnings*

Search for the Missing Hunter by Dave Hart © 2020 iUniverse Publishing, Inc.

Trenton: *a novel* by John P. Calu and David A. Hart Copyright © 2010 Plexus Publishing, Inc.

For more information about Dave Hart's work visit-
https://hartcalu.com/

http://www.plexuspublishing.com/Books/Trenton.shtml

Film/Video
http://www.johnhartpatriot.com/HART/John_Hart.html

https://www.youtube.com/watch?v=10-5j7mzA14

https://www.youtube.com/watch?v=DOLKLEu8Vms

Music
http://www.wavesonamillpond.com/index.html

For my sister, Barbara, an angel incarnate,
and her husband Bob, my friend and concert buddy

Acknowledgments

A very special thanks goes to my
indefatigable editor, Victoria Ford.
Her perception and insightfulness adds an
inimitable quality to the process of my efforts.

Back Cover Photo by Kirk Jarvis,
Eleventhour Productions

1

Her Bare Essence arrived before she did. I caught quite a whiff. Reunited with the rest of her, the combination took my breath away. Or maybe it was the Jack Daniels kicking in.

She slid on to the barstool beside me, as smooth and light as a trapeze artist gliding on her aerial swing. She appeared to be the kind of woman who worked at keeping herself looking good – strict diet, regular exercise, little makeup, right clothing choices. It wouldn't have surprised me to learn she was into hot yoga and tantric sex.

She caught me looking at her naked left ring finger that told me she wasn't married. I believed it. Never been married, she added. I believed that, too. She looked to be in her late thirties, but I wasn't about to ask. I had a habit of eyeing up beautiful young brunettes I'd meet at Jake's on a Friday night – but not usually before I was well into my second drink.

Her glacial blue eyes pierced me to the core. They had a look that told me she had a secret. The kind of eyes that could look right through you. She was looking through me now.

The marriage repartee was not the way I usually started a conversation with a good-looking woman I'd just met. But I'd had a long, grueling day at the office, and I was in the mood for a brief "happy ending" kind of night. When she told me her name was Paige Turner, I nearly fell off the barstool trying to control my laughter. I was certain she was jerking my chain.

"What's so funny?" she asked, downing the drink she had brought over from her table. Vodka and tonic with a twist. The lime rind was a dead giveaway. *Not too shabby*, I thought. Smooth and refreshing – and the drink was real nice, too. A complementary package.

"Your name," I replied with a smirk.

I couldn't tell if the face she made was one of indignation or something else. Either way, she wasn't laughing.

She turned to face me squarely. "What about it?"

"You're kidding, right? That's not really your name."

"What's wrong with my name?"

"It's a play on words, 'page turner.' Like reading a good book. One you just can't put down."

"What can I say? I've been told I'm hard to put down once I've been opened."

"Your father must have a unique sense of humor."

"He has none. He's a novelist," she deadpanned, expecting me to understand the connection.

Turner. The name didn't ring a bell. "Would I have read something by him?"

"I didn't say he was a successful novelist."

"So it *is* your name."

"You want to see my ID?"

"I can vouch that she's old enough," said Nick Falcone, the charming bartender eavesdropping on our conversation.

Nick had the gracefully aging face and youthful head of blond hair of an ex-soap opera actor. He was, in another life – along with other, more nefarious occupations. Bartending was the one he excelled in, mainly because of the revolving array of women it provided him.

He set in front of me another Jack Daniels, neat. Usually, I took my Jack on the rocks, as Nick well knew. Without ice, his pours were like getting two drinks for the price of one. No dilution. Like any experienced bartender used to reading people, he had probably gauged from my scowl when I walked in that I needed to get wasted, pronto.

"I can see you two are settling in. Care for menus?"

"To the contrary," I said, "we're only just getting acquainted. Come back later, would you?"

He set down the lady's refreshed drink. "In that case, play nice," Nick teased, heading off to serve another thirsty customer.

"My apologies," I offered, with a mixture of insincerity and faux embarrassment. "You must get that name thing a lot?"

"Not really. More often I get confused for someone else. Apparently, there's a porn star who uses Paige Turner as her stage name. Like it or not, I'm the real deal."

"Porn star?" I said hopefully.

"Is that what you're looking for, Mister...?"

"Cole. McKenzie Cole. Most people call me 'Mac.'" Once properly introduced, I raised my glass in a gentlemanly salute, hoping to be forgiven for sins past and yet to come.

She responded in kind and smiled coyly.

"Actually, I was hoping to meet someone down-to-earth here tonight," I lied.

She didn't miss a beat. "Is Kansas 'earthy' enough for you? Born and raised. Been a lot of places since."

It was my turn to look at her squarely. "Hard miles, huh? They don't show."

"Trust me, they're there. Comes with the turf."

"In cow country?"

"When you get *steered* into a life of journalism. You're always on the go."

"Now I know you're joking. Paige Turner is a writer too?"

"Yup. It's true what they say. 'The apple doesn't fall far from the tree.'"

"Yes, but if you leave the apple unattended, it might spoil."

"Point taken."

"So, what brings you to our fair city?"

"An assignment. I heard somewhere that Trenton has the lowest crime rates of any medium-sized city in North America. You knocked Topeka off that pedestal recently, and my editor wants to know how."

"That can't be right."

"You're saying *U.S. News and World Report* is wrong?"

"They must mean some other Trenton. For example. There's one in Canada. Near Lake Ontario. I've been there. Now there's a town full of hope and promise."

"Does that Trenton have an African American police chief like your Bill Perkins?"

"Don't know. But when I visited there back in the nineties, they had a mayor by the name of Parks I met. He was black as midnight. Sold life insurance on the side. Apparently, being the top government official in Trenton, Ontario was not all that lucrative."

"Maybe it was, and you just didn't know it. Selling life insurance could have been a cover."

"Now you sound like a reporter."

"We prefer the term 'investigative journalist.'"

"What's the angle?"

"You know Bill Perkins, right? Heard he runs a tight ship."

"To go along with his tight ass," I joked. Truth was Chief Perkins and I had started out as what she might call frenemies. We later found out we worked well together, when mutual interests demanded. But no one cares about hearing the truth, especially nosy investigative journalists. "Let's not talk shop, shall we? After all, it's Friday night."

I was tempted to sip my Jack but instead downed it in one satisfying gulp to emphasize the point. I'm here to drink. Conversation closed. Not very mannerly of me, but, what the hell? I wasn't out to impress. Just to get laid.

She gave me a sympathetic look with those liquid baby blues. "You seem wound-up tonight. What is it that *you* do, Mac?"

"Ah, no fair. No shop talk, remember?"

"Well, at least tell me what you do. I told you."

"He's a private dick," interjected Nick, rushing in to refill my drink.

"Aren't all dicks more or less kept private, until called to attention?" she added without any sense of discomfiture.

"I'm an investigator," I corrected her, shooting Nick a "beat it" glance. "Kinda like you. Only, I don't publish my findings in the newspaper. I keep them private."

"Do you like what you do?"

"Depends on the case. It's a living."

"I imagine you get your share of extramarital philandering and chauffer jobs, since there doesn't appear to be a lot of criminal activity around here that needs to be investigated."

I don't normally get indignant when there's a lady talking, but this bird was trying my patience, denigrating my town and my line of work. That's not the direction I wanted our conversation to go. "I thought we were off duty for the night."

"Oops, right. Sorry. Guess now I'm the one who needs to apologize." She sipped her drink.

As I waited in the intervening pause to catch Nick's eye to refresh Paige's drink, her vibrating cell phone skidded across the bar. She picked it up, looked at the display, and let out a sigh.

"Excuse me, Mac. I have to take this call," she said, slipping from the bar. She put the phone to one ear and a finger in the other as she scurried away from the noisy bar and booming music courtesy of the heavily mascaraed Holly and the Headliners on stage.

Nick placed a coaster in front of me. "Thought you might need to slow the pace a bit," he explained. "Don't tell me the Cole charm's not working its magic tonight?"

Nick hit the nail on the head. A wall separated us. Call it professional differences. It was beginning to feel like an occupational hazard to me. "Ever see her in here before, Nick?"

"Can't say I have. A real looker. I'd remember."

"I'm sure you would. Says she's just passing through. A journalist on assignment."

"Sounds like the perfect one-night stand, if you get lucky, buddy. Right up your alley."

"Up yours."

We laughed, in that conspiratorial sort of way frat brothers do while planning a rager replete with sorority girls.

Nick grew thoughtful. "Funny – initially I thought you knew her. She came in here asking for you."

"She did?"

"Well, sort of. She wanted to know who in this town knew 'where all the bodies were buried.' So I mentioned your name. Figured in your line of work you come across a lot of secret shit."

I scoffed. "The town gossip, anointing *me* 'in the know'? That's rich."

"Yeah, well. I assumed she was here to bring you some business," Nick explained. "I didn't expect you to chase her away so quickly."

"She got paged," I said, smiling at the pun.

Nick nodded, then lumbered off. Paige returned, looking none too happy.

"Problem?" I inquired.

"That was my editor. He's moved up the deadline for the story I'm working on. Wants it in tomorrow's edition."

"Can he do that?"

"He just did. Peters is a prick. But he's a damn good editor. He has a nose for news."

She shrugged on her coat and reached into her purse to pay for her drink. I stopped her.

"You don't need to do that," she said.

"Shall I save the seat?" I asked, sounding more sheepish than I meant to.

"Not tonight," she said.

"Right. Tomorrow then."

"We'll see."

"How long are you in town?"

"That depends."

"Depends on what?"

"My assignment."

2

....

"What the hell did you tell her?"

I held my cell phone at arm's length. Chief Perkins was mad as a hornet. I was certain my secretary could hear him shouting beyond the closed office door.

"Who?" I asked naively. It was nine a.m. on a working Saturday, and I still hadn't settled into my morning routine. My hangover fog remained thick.

"That female reporter who tracked you down at Jake's last night."

"Turner? Hey, I struck out, if you must know. In fact, I don't think we were in the same ballpark. Why? What did she say? Is she pressing charges?"

"Didn't you see this morning's paper?"

On cue, my ever-efficient secretary, "Mother" Mary Porter, stood at my desk, holding up the daily rag so I could see the headline: **Trenton Police Under Investigation; Chief on Temporary Leave.**

Perkins continued his tirade. "The mayor thought an administrative leave would lower the temperature until Internal Affairs could wrap their arms around the allegations," Perkins said, as though reading the headline along with me.

8

From our brief conversation, I couldn't recall anything that might implicate Trenton's "boys in blue" in criminal misconduct, unless occasionally accepting free doughnuts fell into that category. "Bill, what's this got to do with me?"

"The bitch quotes an unidentified source."

"And you think I'm that source?"

"Falcone told us you were drinking with her at the bar."

That snake. Nick enjoyed playing the prankster between us. He was what's known as a "mixer" in merry old England, and I wasn't referring to his stock in trade. "I bought her one drink. So?"

"That devil drink of yours has been known to loosen your tongue from time to time."

The insinuation stuck. Just ask my ex-wife. "Bill, you're barking up the wrong tree. Turner was in town for one night. The story had to be in the works well before she got here."

"You seem to know quite a bit about her schedule."

"Only what she shared with me. I know even less about your police affairs."

"Your disdain for O'Malley is common knowledge around here."

That was true. Over the years, I had had my run-ins with Detective Greg O'Malley and was not shy about criticizing him. But that had everything to do with his sloppy police work and caustic personality – not criminal behavior. I never accused him of any wrongdoing. Besides, the feeling was mutual. He looked down at me and people in my profession. "Bottom feeders," he called us. Thing is, the bottom is where the buried treasure is.

"So, what are the charges? Embezzlement? Graft? Wife swapping?"

"Underreporting serious crimes to the Crime Bureau."

"That's a crime? Doesn't every precinct in the U.S. do that?"

"Whose side are you on?"

"You know that's ridiculous, Bill. It'll never stand up in court."

"Yeah, tell me about it. Except when it's intended to mislead the public, it's considered corruption. And that's damning."

"The mayor of Topeka must exercise a lot of influence over the press."

"Say again?"

"That journalist works for the *Kansas City Sun Times*. Her work gets picked up by the Associated Press. Topeka has long been known as a peaceful place to raise kids, with solid law enforcement. Your group knocked Topeka off the top spot, which it apparently held for years."

"That's bullshit."

"Probably, Bill. But that's what she told me. It does make for a sensational story."

"Sounds like 'yellow journalism' to me."

"Me too. Absolutely scandalous. Where did Trenton place in prior years?"

"I have no idea."

Mary held up two fingers, then three. Apparently, Chief Perkins' voice was still amped up enough for her to hear our ongoing conversation.

"Twenty-third, Bill, according to the article in the paper. What are you doing differently?"

"Covering up arrests, according to your Ms. Turner."

"Doesn't everyone do that, too?"

Perkins let out a deep sigh. "According to the *Star*, only Trenton. And only the murders."

...

"What are you going to do?" Mary asked after I'd hung up the phone with Chief Perkins. He was called away to offer his comments at a press conference being hastily arranged by Mayor Hasbrouck's office.

"Nothing. It's not my fight."

"But he's your friend."

"We're colleagues, Mary. He'd never admit to us being anything more than that."

"Only in public."

"Right. The public is his responsibility. Mine is to mind my own business."

"I can't believe you're not going to help him."

"He doesn't need my help."

"Then why did he call you?"

"He thought I ratted him out."

"He knows you better than that."

"He's grasping at straws."

"He's asking for your help."

Mary had been with me since I started my investigative business four years ago, after being unceremoniously let go from my previous employer in the wake of a hostile takeover by a foreign conglomerate. She had left a comfortable position with that same employer because she believed in me. She had given up a job that included health insurance and a good pension, for mere pocket change. In all that time, she had been my one and only employee, and my confidante when my better angels flew south. At times, Mary could work on my psyche better than my own mother. Now was one of those times.

"What can I do to help him?"

"Find the female reporter. Get to the truth."

"That may not be easy. Suppose she's left town. I wouldn't know where to begin."

"Start where it began."

I stared at her blankly, waiting for the prosaic punchline I knew would follow.

"Start with Nick Falcone."

3

· · · · · · · · · · · ·

I hated when Mary Porter was right, as she proved time and time again. I expected it this time. But for once, I got it right, too.

I found Nick at his workplace, the venerable Jake's Joint on South Broad and Clinton, hanging clean wine glasses on the rack above the bar and flirting with Holly of the Headliners fame.

It was two in the afternoon. The place smelled of sawdust and beer. Holly was savoring a rum and coke while waiting for the rest of the band to arrive for a run-through of tonight's show. Without her long blonde locks, thick mascara and skin-tight black leather, Holly looked like the girl next door. And I do mean *girl*, although by Nick's account she was a very experienced twenty-eight-year-old. A vixen with a golden voice reminiscent of a gritty Stevie Nicks, a scorching Pat Benatar, or my personal favorite, a down and dirty Melissa Etheridge. Take your pick. All of them fit the persona she wove herself around, which made me think of her as the chameleon songstress, of which a man like me would never tire.

Holly blew Nick a kiss, then blew me off, as she moved on over to the stage where a buffed and bald roadie in a torn vintage Headliners tee was checking the sound levels coming through the amplifiers.

"What's up, Mac?" Nick greeted me with his choirboy smile. "You and Perkins still friends?"

"We never were friends. And thanks to you, we never will be. What were you thinking?"

"When I read the paper this morning, I felt a civic duty to relate what I knew. Perkins is a patron, too. And he tips better than you. There was something off about that woman. You said so yourself."

"You made me out to be a co-conspirator. I barely spoke to her."

"No, man. I swear. That's just how Perkins interpreted it."

"Whatever, Nick. What's done is done. You can make amends by helping me locate her. I assume she left town this morning. Do you know where she was staying?"

"Don't you?"

"You saw me. I didn't get to first base."

"Oh, right."

"How about a number? I guess we could always try the *Sun Times*. Unless you pulled your usual schtick and —"

"Nah, man. It was a busy night. I didn't get the chance."

"Okay. She ordered a drink, though, right? Then sat at that table to wait for me."

"Right."

"Did she pay with cash or use a card?"

"Card, as I recall. You're the only one who pays with cash these days, Mac. It's a Boomer thing."

"You got the receipt?"

"It should still be in the drawer. Jake has me remove the cash from the register and put it in the safe when I close up. But I generally leave the receipts for when he comes in around four. Lemme check."

As Nick hurried off, I cased the empty joint carefully. The band and a few lunch patrons milled around sluggishly. The place looked very different in the daytime. Not at all the comforting watering hole I'd come to rely on more than enjoy. Still Nick threw a lot of business my way with his bar connections, so I couldn't stay mad at him forever.

"Here you go." He handed me the scrap of paper. The printing was small and smudged but readable. The only information I could make use of was her signature. At least it matched the name she gave me and the byline on that morning's exposé.

"Probably a business credit card," Nick mused. "I see them all the time."

"Yeah. Thanks."

Nick tossed a Michelob coaster on the bar in front of me.

"It's a little early," I said, thinking he was about to pour me a Jack on the rocks.

"Turn it over."

On the reverse side was a phone number beginning with a 785 area code, in the same neat handwriting as the signed credit card receipt.

Nick shrugged and gave me an "aw, shucks" grin. "I had her give me her number in case you didn't make it in last night."

I chuckled. Yeah right, no chance in hell that was what happened.

"Anyway, now we're even," he said with his charismatic wink.

4

. . . .

Turns out 785 was not an area code for Kansas City, according to my trusty secretary's internet sleuthing after the number Nick passed on to me turned out to be disconnected. I should have known a wolf like Nick would meet his match in a sharp woman like Paige Turner. But 785 was the area code for Topeka, Kansas, which only heightened the mystery.

The resourceful Mary Porter conducted a reverse phone number lookup, which led her to a Martin L. Turner in Topeka. Whether he was Paige's husband, father or brother, we could not say. But an online search confirmed Martin Turner was author of the less-than-stirring true crime novel *Dark Mercy*, along with various other titles. Born in 1962, he married a Cornelia "Connie" King in 1984 and embarked on a military stint that included action in Operation Desert Storm. He and Connie had a son named Penrose and a daughter named Paige, both born August 15, 1986. Twin siblings, still living! Connie and Martin divorced in 1993, shortly after *Dark Mercy* was published and panned. I picked up the phone and dialed.

A gruff male voice answered.

"If you're looking for my daughter, she's not here."

"Martin Turner?"

"Who wants to know?"

"I'm an acquaintance of hers."

"So you say."

"Can I leave a message?"

"What do you think, I'm her messenger service?"

"Is she still in Trenton?"

"How the hell should I know? Call her editor. Gary Peters. *Sun Times.*"

CLICK.

That went well. With the story running over every wire service in the country and her line disconnected, he must be inundated with prank calls. I'd be pissed, too. I didn't even get a chance to tell him how much I admired his work. I made a mental note to mention that during our next call.

I found the number for the *Kansas City Sun Times*, but before I could make the call, Mary buzzed me. "Mac, Chief Perkins is on line one."

"Put him through."

But instead of Perkins, a quavering female voice came on the line.

"Sorry for the deception, Mac."

It was Shirley Mae Brown, the plump and vociferous Trenton Police dispatcher who also just happened to bake the best cornbread this side of the Delaware.

"What's wrong, Shirley Mae?"

"It's the chief. He doesn't know I'm calling you."

"How is he?"

"That's just it. We don't know where he is. He left the station after the press conference without a word to anyone."

"So, who is running the department?"

Silence.

"Shirley Mae?"

"O'Malley."

"You're shitting me! Whose hairbrained idea was that?"

"His."

"Bill's?"

"Yes, and Hasbrouck approved it."

"Because O'Malley has seniority?"

"Because he's head of the detective division. He's the senior staff member."

"That just means he's the last man standing in that division."

"Mac, you've got to do something. Headquarters is in turmoil."

"What can I do?"

"Get to the bottom of it. Find where this stuff is coming from."

"Did Perkins ask you to reach out to me?"

Silence again.

"Shirley Mae?"

"No. We are acting on our own."

"O'Malley, too?"

"No."

"Then it's not official."

"No one has to know about it."

"Internal Affairs won't like it. You should let them do their job."

"They won't do nothin'. We can pay you, Mac. We all agreed to take up a collection through the PBA if we must. Name your price."

The desperation in her voice was heartbreaking. The folks around Bill Perkins were as loyal to him as he was to them, with more than twenty years of service as their unquestioned leader. He was a straight shooter who led by example. I'd seen him in action many times. Confident, efficient, and totally committed.

"That's not the issue, here, Shirley Mae, and you know it."

"Mac, O'Malley doesn't have to know."

"Who has access to the crime bureau's report filings?"

"The chief."

"So O'Malley will have access as acting chief."

"He wants no part of the investigation, Mac. He's letting IA have free rein. He's delegated the whole thing to them so he can concentrate on the day-to-day stuff."

"How do you know this?"

"They've asked me and a few of the other dispatchers to pull the records for them."

"Can you make copies?"

"Does a bear shit in the woods?"

"Great."

"Get what you can on the QT – and, Shirley Mae?"

"Yes?"

"Don't get caught. You could lose your job."

With the conversation concluded, I buzzed Mary, who was listening in. "You heard?"

"Every word."

"You know it's probably going to be a pro bono case."

"Some causes just feel right."

"They don't pay the mortgage, Mary."

"When has that ever stopped you?"

"You must have a very understanding bank."

"They know who I work for."

"Shirley Mae will be taking a hell of a risk."

"She's a big girl. With an even bigger heart, which is in the right place, Mac. So is yours."

"I guess we'd better get to work, then."

5

. . . .

I had the pleasure of rummaging through police records myself, once. In a cold-case murder that had gone unsolved some forty years. I found the law enforcement files were not always neat and tidy, even in this digital day and age.

I didn't know anything about the National Crime Bureau, nor which federal agency was responsible for compiling and housing the data. A quick Google search sent me in the right direction. It fell under the jurisdiction of Department of Justice. Bureau of Justice Statistics was the lofty moniker for the section tasked with the responsibility.

As expected, the data was not for the current year or even the prior year. Compiling archival data from literally thousands of precincts scattered across the United States takes years to collect. Requiring forbearance and patience, the task is tedious, to put it mildly. In this particular case the latest statistics were from 2020, which made the data two-and-a-half years old!

In the big scheme of things, the Bureau of Justice Statistics' primary role was data collection, functioning as a central warehouse where information was stored, parsed, and distributed to various organizations like *U.S. News and World Report* for analysis and reporting as they saw fit. The main concern for all seemed to be drilling down to law enforcement's "bang for the buck" on a state-by-state basis, as measured in per capita expenditures. Other conclusions drawn from the results, such as crime-free zones, safest places to live or retire, and/or judicial efficacy, were secondary considerations, often with misinterpreted or misleading conclusions.

Getting my hands on the half-cocked conclusions of the *U.S. News* article would be easy. Getting my hands on the data dump at the Bureau of Justice Statistics would not be. Nor would obtaining the allegedly hidden, doctored, or misfiled reports of the Trenton Police Department. For that I would need to see the source materials. Lucky for me, I had an inside man – er, gal – already on the job.

More important, I needed to talk to someone at the *Kansas City Sun Times*, either Paige Turner or her editor, about the investigative process that led to the publication of their sensational story, along with the timing of it. The *U.S. News* article was nearly four months old. When released, it basically flew under everyone's radar, although, admittedly, seeing Trenton named "safest mid-level population city in America" was a real eye-opener, especially given its mediocre standing in prior listings.

Had I known any of this would be forthcoming following our innocent and brief encounter at Jake's, I would have been more alert and attentive. Maybe the meeting wasn't so innocent. Nick did say Paige Turner had come in looking for me. How did she know Jake's was my "home away from home," so to speak? Evidently, she was tipped off by someone. But who, and for what purpose?

Even with half a snoot on, surely I didn't and wouldn't say anything derogatory about Trenton's finest or Chief Perkins personally. Whether I knew I was being interviewed or not. That would be bad for business. I have to work with the boys in blue. Besides, I had far more pleasurable things on my mind, which, regrettably, didn't materialize.

All this soul searching left a gaping hole in my rational thinking about the oddness of this case. That, and a bunch of questions. What was so important to the people of Kansas about this story? Topeka had a good run. Why not let some other city have the limelight? What did they have against a sister city like Trenton, anyway?

And what was Paige's purpose in coming to see me? The story was already written before she flew into Trenton. The call from her editor when she was at the bar was unexpected. Sudden. Orders from headquarters! Why the urgency? What was she trying to convey to me?

That's when it hit me: My mental gyrations indeed had a purpose. I knew where I had to go next. If my hunch was correct, that's where I'd find Paige Turner.

6

• • • • • • • • • • •

The clue was in the word "flew" in my mind when I considered *how* rather than *why* Paige Turner came to Trenton. For now, I put aside the "why." That was a conundrum for another day.

Reporter or not, Ms. Turner's refinement and her taste in drink and dress were among the details I recalled from our meeting that were most impressive about her. A smart, sophisticated woman would not travel halfway across the country on her employer's dime by car in the early spring. She'd fly. Especially if time was of the essence, as appeared to be so. She knew the publication of the story was imminent. Days away. Whatever she needed or wanted to communicate to me could not wait.

Trenton-Mercer Airport, located in rural Ewing Township, just off I-95 across from a minimum-security prison farm that raised its own dairy cows, was the northeast hub of the hustling regional Frontier Airlines. Filling a unique and mostly profitable niche, Frontier routinely flew to several out-of-the-way, secondary midwestern cities that major carriers did not, such as Cincinnati, Ohio; Des Moines, Iowa; and Kansas City,

Kansas. The only drawback was the lack of planes to fly to all those small city destinations daily.

The only outgoing flight to Kansas City for today from Trenton-Mercer was set to depart at seven p.m. That gave me an hour to cover the ten-minute drive.

Essentially a commuter airplane hangar dating back to the bleak, Cold-War 1950s, the Trenton-Mercer terminal was repurposed in the '80s when Mercer County sought the additional tax revenue that came with larger airplanes and burgeoning air traffic. In forty years, the volume grew, but the airlines came and went until Frontier finally touched down more or less permanently.

The expansion efforts at the terminal were done piecemeal, to the point where the original hangar had been subdivided into three distinct horizontal sections dictated by function. Closest to the parking lot was check-in, a two-man booth for ticketing. The middle section was cordoned off with velvet rope for baggage handling. The section nearest the runway contained a small lounge for passengers prior to boarding. Above the lounge was a cozy restaurant with a glass mezzanine that overlooked the airfield outside and the lounge below, where loved ones could wave goodbye.

Standing at the mezzanine's railing, I scoured the lounge for a glimpse of the elusive Paige Turner. Apparently, the Kansas City flight was the only scheduled departure, so the terminal was sparsely populated. Spotting Paige Turner would be easy if she was there. She was not.

After all the passengers boarded and the plane took off, I hustled back to the check-in station, where an overweight, pimply-faced twenty-something nerd named Cliff Warren wearing a Frontier uniform was working alone. I waited for an elderly gentleman in front of me to finish, then I moved up to the counter.

"How may I help you?" Cliff inquired, unenthused.

"Can you tell me if you have a passenger named Paige Turner on the flight to Kansas City that just left?"

He frowned. "Are you a cop?"

"My inquiry comes from a higher authority."

"The FBI?"

With my right hand I motioned him to think higher. With my left, I passed him twenty bucks.

He giggled. "Cool." He glanced around, took a step to his left to block the security camera with his shoulder and pocketed the twenty.

Looking at his computer screen, he continued, "She was supposed to be on that flight. Seat 8F. But she canceled her reservation."

"When?"

"Sometime today."

"Did she book another flight?"

"Nope. The return portion of her roundtrip ticket is still open. It's an option we give our gold-level frequent flyers. They have thirty days to fill it or pay the transfer fee when they do."

Gold level, my ass. That might earn you a bag of peanuts and a neck cushion. Given the sales pitch, I decided to press my luck. "Does your computer provide contact information for Ms. Turner? Like a number in case you need to reach her about her flight status?"

Cliffy smiled, stretching his face until his pimples were about to burst. "Your higher authority's records don't have that info?"

Smartass. "Tell you what. I'll give you what we do have. All you have to do is verify it hasn't changed. Fair enough?"

I didn't wait for a reply. From memory, I spat out Martin Turner's disconnected phone number that Paige had given to Nick the bartender and he gave to me.

Smirking, Cliff said, "Yeah, that's the one."

"Cool," I said, sliding another twenty-dollar bill across the counter. "Anything else?"

In one motion, he glanced up at the security camera and swiped the twenty. He tapped a few keys. A printer under the counter whirred into gear. Reaching under the counter, he tore off the printed paper, folded it and placed it into a boarding pass envelope along with Gold Card member info.

Handing the envelope to me, he added sarcastically, "Thanks for flying Frontier!"

Turns out old Cliffy was not as dumb as he looked. On the printout he had typed, "Next time, fly Delta!"

Sound advice, given the first-class service I'd gotten from Frontier.

I sat in the airport parking lot, pondering my next move. I consoled myself with the thought that my forty-dollar investment into Frontier Cliff's retirement pension wasn't a total loss. I'd learned that Paige Turner was originally scheduled for the seven-p.m. flight to Kansas City but had changed her mind suddenly. Also, if Cliff's passenger info could be trusted, Paige had not yet booked her return flight.

That meant she was still in town. Why? Was it the McKenzie Cole charm that persuaded her to stay? Even my overinflated ego couldn't buy that. Maybe her staying didn't have anything to do with me. After all, she had a full day and made no attempt to contact me. Was she simply lying low, gauging the local fallout caused by her sensational story? That could mean she was gathering material for the follow-up story: how things played out in Trenton after the shakedown of the Trenton Police Department.

The mind of an investigative reporter was difficult enough to understand. A woman, too? I felt like a participant in a double-blind experiment. And I wasn't comfortable with that at all.

7

· · · · · · · · · · · ·

"Peters is a prick."

For some reason that phrase stuck with me. I didn't understand its meaning at the time when she said it. But suddenly it came back to me. Although attempts to reach him during the day by phone proved frustrating, I now knew who he was. While his role in the whole wild story might seem a given, to me it remained a loose thread that needed tying up.

I glanced at my watch. Eight p.m. local time. That meant six p.m. in Kansas City. With any luck I'd catch Peters before he left for the day. As city editor he might stick around to oversee the printing of the evening edition. Just about this time yesterday, Paige Turner had taken his urgent call at the bar, spoiling our night and complicating my day.

I dialed. Nine rings in, I was ready to hang up, when a gruff male voice answered. "City desk. Peters."

"Trenton Central. Perkins." It was a cheap shot. But I figured two could play this game.

Silence, followed by a slow midwestern tone.

"Z'at right. What do you want?"

"I want you to know you'll be hearing from my lawyer."

"Already have. Got nothing to say to you."

"Then maybe you want me talk to your reporter, Turner." Another shot in the dark.

"Go ahead. You'll get nothing from her. Our sources are protected."

"We'll see. Put her on."

Peters chuckled. "Yeah, right."

"Then relay a message to her. If she ever comes to Trenton, we'll have her arrested."

"On what charge?"

"Disturbing the peace."

"Yeah, guess her piece is causing quite a disturbance around your parts today. Better call the police."

A real wiseass. Even if I was the one masquerading as the police chief, Peters was starting to get under my skin. It was time to call his bluff.

"You realize you have nothing."

"The bodies will eventually turn up."

Suddenly the din on the line grew louder as the newspaper presses began rolling.

"It's been nice chatting with you, Perkins. Gotta go. I've got a paper to run."

He didn't wait for my rejoinder. Frankly, I had none. Fact was, I was ruminating on what he had said just before the presses sputtered to life. *The bodies will turn up.* That sounded eerily like the line Paige Turner had thrown to Nick Falcone – the comment, based on his retelling, that got me ensnared in this mess in the first place.

She wanted to know *who knew where all the bodies were buried.* I thought it was a throwaway line, something said to strike up conversation. Coming from a journalist, it seemed quite natural. Reporters were always digging for a story.

But maybe there was more to it, something behind the numbers. I picked up the newspaper lying on the passenger seat of my Jaguar and slowly re-read Paige Turner's front page story.

8

· · · · · · · · · · · ·

True to her word, Shirley Mae Brown was out of uniform and in my office before working an overtime shift Sunday to assist Internal Affairs on their investigation. She was out of uniform, I suppose, to appear off-duty while she delivered her initial National Crime Bureau report findings to me. I asked Mary to sit in with us and take notes.

Normally genial and gregarious, Shirley today seemed a little nervous. That was unlike the big-hearted Shirley I knew, who went out of her way to be helpful to nearly everyone. She sat in an armchair in front of me with her legs crossed, her left foot tapping to an unknown beat. To be sure, I was not used to seeing the plump Trenton police dispatcher in street clothes. Out of her khakis and pressed blue shirt she appeared a little beefier than usual. Like a butterball turkey.

"Whatcha got for us?" I asked in a normal tone, hoping to calm her nerves.

"Well, I ain't seen everything yet, but what I have seems a little odd to me, 'specially the violent crime filings."

"What's odd about them?"

"There ain't any!" she blurted right out.

"What constitutes a 'violent crime'?" I asked innocently, although I was pretty sure I knew.

"Duh. How 'bout murder, for one."

Again, I played innocent. "And zero's unusual for Trenton?"

"Hell, Mac, we've got a dozen already this year, and it's only May."

"What does Internal Affairs think? Do they find it odd, too?"

"Nope. They say, you gots to remember, 2020 was the year of the COVID-19 pandemic. Nobody went nowhere. Bars were closed. Travel was restricted. People worked from their homes."

"That makes sense. Can't get into too many scrapes if you're not out and about."

"What about domestic violence?" Mary offered. "Couples cooped up together twenty-four-seven for months on end. That'll strain any relationship."

"Do we know the number of murders for Topeka in 2020?"

Mary put down her steno pad and flipped open to the chart. "Two."

I turned back to Shirley. "There you go."

"Shit, Mac. I was there in 2020. I took the calls. Ain't no way we got through a whole year without a single murder."

That did seem obvious. Perhaps we'd sent ours to Topeka. "What about Perkins? What's the chief say about that?"

"Nobody can find him. It's like he's abandoned us. Just walked away."

"That's not his style, Shirley Mae. We both know it."

"Then why don't he come out to defend himself? Defend the force?"

"I can't explain his intentions any more than I can explain his sudden disappearance. Have you tried calling his cell phone?"

"We all have. He don't answer it."

Mary stopped writing. "Or can't."

On that note, Shirley Mae stood up. "I gots to go. Don't want to be late. O'Malley might suspect something."

"How's old Greg boy now that he's in charge?"

"Man's a Sphinx. A total mystery. Ain't nothing rattles him no more. Just hanging on until he can collect his pension."

I know the type. Detective Gregory O'Malley definitely fit the mold. Twenty-plus years on the force. Maybe two to go until retirement. Divorced. Kids grown. No girlfriends. No hobbies except to make my life miserable whenever we met. "Lucky us," I deadpanned.

"Hmph!" exclaimed Shirley. "I'll be in touch."

At the door, Shirley stopped abruptly. Turning back, she spoke directly: "I ain't supposed to know this. Nobody is. So don't ask me how I know. But I hear tell Chief Perkins is an avid fisherman, and that he gots hisself a little fishing shack down in Tuckerton where he goes from time to time, you know, to forget who he is and what he does for a living."

I knew Bill Perkins liked to fish. At least, I knew he liked to order fish at restaurants whenever we ate out together. Which wasn't often. But I'd never heard him boast about his prowess with rod and reel. So, Shirley Mae's admission came as a complete surprise to me. I knew better than to ask her how she knew, but I thought I would chance one more question. "Do you know where it is, exactly?"

A wry smile formed on her chubby face. "Yeah. On the water."

...

Shirley Mae had handed me a challenge. I didn't know which was more surprising – that Bill Perkins had a passion for fishing and a secret hideaway, or that Shirley Mae knew about it. Given my training as an insurance underwriter and experience as a claims investigator, I had a hunch I could locate the former. As for the latter, I had a sneaking suspicion, and I didn't want to know anything more about it.

Bill Perkins was a complicated man, and a very private one, as anyone with his responsibilities must be. I, for one, did not want to go poking my nose into his business. Nor did I want to disturb the hornet's nest. Shirley Mae had twice given me very little wiggle room to back away from either invitation.

"I know that look," said Mary, interrupting my thoughts.

"What look?"

"Face squeeze. Then you stroke your bushy mustache. It means you're going to go looking for Chief Perkins."

"I have no choice. Shirley Mae threw down the gauntlet."

"What if Chief Perkins doesn't want to be found?"

"That's the puzzling part. Why is he hiding? What's he hiding?"

"Do you think O'Malley knows about the fishing shack?"

"I doubt it. The two aren't very close. Barely speak to one another, apart from professional courtesy."

Mary seemed perplexed. "Why is that? Something happen between them?"

"I think at one time, early in his career, O'Malley fancied himself stepping into the position Perkins eventually got and has held for over twenty years. That must have been tough for O'Malley to swallow. My guess is he suspects there were some sensitive political maneuverings involved. When you look at the demographics of the city in the '80s and '90s, there was, and still is, a significant ethnic constituency to mollify. O'Malley was on the losing end, and, in his mind, not for lack of experience or ability. Back then he may have been correct. But Bill Perkins has proven himself to be the right man for the job, time and time again. No question."

"Given what you just said, doesn't it seem strange that Perkins would, after all these years, pick him even temporarily to be his replacement?"

"Absolutely, Mary. Bill's no dummy though. I can only presume he has his reasons. And that they are very good reasons."

9

· · · · · · · · · · · ·

Despite interpretations to the contrary, Tuckerton in Ocean County is technically not a New Jersey shore town. It's located on the mainland, across Great Bay from the southern tip of Long Beach Island, or LBI, as it is known. Once called 'Clam Town' for the industry that fueled its economy, Tuckerton clams fed patrons of the finest Manhattan restaurants, transforming the small hamlet into a tourist destination.

Rich in history and lore, Tuckerton played a critical role in the American Revolution by supplying George Washington's Continental Army with European goods provided by privateers and merchant seaman. For a period, when British warships closed the major ports of New York and Philadelphia, Tuckerton notoriously became the largest mid-Atlantic port capable of importing contraband.

Essentially a fishing village with navigable waters far inland, Tuckerton remained a sportsman's paradise for fishing, crabbing, clamming, and duck hunting in season. Fishermen here were easy to find. A police chief hiding out and posing as a fisherman? Well, that idea was crazier than hell. But that's exactly what I set out to do.

Several routes would take me to Tuckerton. Almost any New Jersey town could be reached by the Garden State Parkway, if you knew what exit to take, going north or south. But traveling eastward from Trenton on the Delaware River, the best route by far was 539 through the Pine Barrens.

Any time I could take my vintage metallic blue 1966 Jaguar XKE for a ride on the open road with the top down was an exhilarating day for me. And this was one of those days. A glorious hour and a half later, I was on Main Street (Route 9) at the Tuckerton Seaport, having coffee and consulting a map of the town with the knowledgeable and amiable Lighthouse Museum Director, Becky Gibson, a lifelong Tuckerton resident.

I told her I had just come from the municipal tax office, which was closed because it was Sunday. Running out of options, I asked her if she could help.

She explained the database of property tax records was online and proceeded to look it up. Unfortunately, she came up blank for any properties belonging to a Perkins.

She then told me Main Street had a mix of commercial and residential properties, most of them with occupants Becky knew personally from activities in town and at the Seaport, and none of whom were named Perkins or fit the description.

For weekend and summer fishing enthusiasts she said my best bet was to look at the upscale – for Tuckerton, anyway – community off of Radio Road known as Mystic Islands. This manmade expanse was backfilled, built upon and bordered by lagoons for easy water access for fishermen and boaters. When I inquired about the possibility of an isolated shack on the lagoon in the Mystic

Islands, Becky's face contorted like a pretzel. "You mean like those tarpaper shacks in the Pines?"

"I don't know," I admitted. "The person who gave me the information said the person I'm looking for could be found in Tuckerton, in a fishing shack, 'on the water.' Where do I begin? There's water everywhere around here!"

Becky scanned the map. "Perhaps she meant literally *on the water*," she said. "Maybe something like a houseboat in the area off Great Bay Boulevard.

"Aren't houseboats basically trailers on pontoons?"

"Some people find them sexy. Inexpensive and very practical for sportsmen coming in for the weekend, from Philadelphia or Trenton."

"Is the area around Great Bay remote? Because it would need to be."

"It's mostly marshland. Land access is limited to a single gravel lane that juts out into the Bay. The road, if you can call it that, is connected to each island by a series of rickety wooden bridges. The final bridge was never completed because the project ran out of money back in the days just before the Depression. Now it is used mostly by fishermen, crabbers and a few naturalists who study the habitats of the ospreys, herons and snowy white egrets. On a clear day you can see the Atlantic City skyline, if that's of any interest to you."

That sounds like my kind of place, I assured her. She briefed me on directions, adding, "You might want to wait until morning to start your search. You only have about an hour or so of good daylight left. There is unreliable electricity running along Great Bay Boulevard. Just enough to power the one-way traffic signals over the narrow wooden bridges. And no streetlights. Driving there can be hazardous at night if you don't know the road."

"I like to live dangerously," I said with a devilish smile.

She walked me to the door and gasped in obvious delight at the sight of my classy Jaguar. "If you're going in that beautiful thing, you should at least put the top up. It can get mighty buggy at night, out there on the marshes."

"I'll risk it," I said.

"Well, good luck, then," she added with a hesitant wave.

Luck was not what I needed. Stealth, maybe. Or a miracle. My odds of finding Bill Perkins were little better than finding a needle in the haystack. I wasn't counting on seeing his name scrawled on a mailbox, but I was hoping I might spot his maroon Chevy Silverado parked outside a shack or near his docked houseboat. His might not be the only truck of its kind in Tuckerton. But surely it would be the only one with the vanity plate BIG BLU 1.

Night falls fast when you're in a convertible on a lonely stretch of road in the Pine Barrens, surrounded by water. Darkness envelops you like a blanket over a casket, both in terms of the solitude and the deathly silence. That's precisely the way I was feeling: alone and apart from the world. If Bill Perkins wanted seclusion, this was the place.

The drive reminded me of a road trip I took with my ex-wife in happier days, down Highway A1A to Key West. It was the year after our wedding. We were on our first real vacation as husband and wife, excluding our thrift-minded honeymoon to LBI. On this trip we were staying at the luxury hotel Fontainebleau in Miami Beach.

Beth and I had decided to be adventurous and just wing it in our rented Chrysler Le Baron convertible. We drove with the top down, wind in our hair. Not a care in the world.

The road was flat, seemingly at sea level, with the Atlantic Ocean on our left and the Caribbean Sea on our right – neither more than eight feet away from the car doors. It was a bit terrifying but picturesque.

We reached Key West as the sun was setting. After a quick drink at Sloppy Joe's, Hemingway's fabled watering hole, we followed the boisterous crowd and hurried off to the wharf to catch one of those spectacular Key West sunsets you read about in travel brochures.

I should have known then it was a sign of things to come. Trouble seemed to follow us, lying in wait to unravel upon us at the worst time. An ocean liner had stayed too long in port, so when the tide rolled out, the steamer was left stranded in the shallows. Blocks long, the massive ship spoiled the occasion by blotting out the entire sunset view.

Undeterred, we checked into a nearby Days Inn and hustled back to Sloppy Joe's for a nightcap (or three). The following two days rained; Key West was a washout for us. We headed back to Miami in the Le Baron with the top up and our heads down, while water crested just outside our car doors.

Our best laid plans always ended up in disappointment for one reason or another. We couldn't always blame it on the weather or a ship that should've sailed but didn't. Certainly, our timing was off on a great many things, jobs, pets, kids. Over the years, as we grew further apart, our marriage suffered.

These morbid thoughts held my attention as I crept up and down Great Bay Boulevard in search of Perkins' hideaway. Along the way, as I waited my turn to cross one narrow bridge after another, fishermen waved and marveled at my car as I drove by. I counted five bridges in total.

"Any luck?" I shouted to an elder angler as I passed inches from his chum bucket, holding the day's catch.

"Nothing like yours, young fella," he quipped. "But I'll trade you what's in this here bucket for them wheels, if you're interested."

No thanks, old man. Get real. This car was the only thing of value I had left after my divorce settlement. She didn't want it because it had been in an accident – a vehicular homicide involving a young boy. The insurance company I worked for at the time was glad to part with it at any price. So, yeah, you might say I made a deal with the devil. I cashed in on one death and held onto to it as I watched my marriage die.

By now the sun had indeed set, and I was running low on fuel and patience. I'd spotted a couple of houseboats, but they appeared rundown and uninhabited. It was time to head back to civilization. I needed a cold drink, a hot shower, and a soft, warm bed – with or without any female toppings.

I made a K-turn at the at the end of the final linked island in the chain. Beyond it lay the submerged remnants of a famous sandbar once known as Tucker's Island, an occasional hazard to boaters, and beyond that, the Beach Haven inlet and the wide-open Atlantic Ocean.

Driving back, a car approached with its high beams on. One of only a handful of vehicles I'd seen the entire time I traversed the long narrow road. Though at times my paranoia told me I was being followed at a distance by a silver Nissan Rogue.

I flashed the other driver as a warning, but the lights kept coming. The signal should have stopped traffic on the other side of the bridge. I had the right of way, the green light.

It was that same silver Rogue. We were playing chicken with nowhere to go. I flashed again but got no response. So, I put on my brights, hoping to get my message across.

No dice. The SUV bore down. Quickly I assessed my situation and calculated my odds. This bozo either was impaired or meant to ram me. Our lights clashed. I felt targeted.

It was darker now. Sand crunched beneath my tires. The moon glistened on the water. I couldn't tell how much room I had on either side, or whether it was gravel or marsh.

Onward. Not fast enough to cause severe injury, but reckless and potentially damaging to my Jag. Too valuable to risk. I pulled off to the shoulder of the road and screeched to a stop, praying I'd stay aground.

The Rogue swept past me, not even breaking as it plowed over the sloping embankment and plunked into the bay.

I leapt out of my car and ran toward the sinking Rogue. Something was terribly wrong. No driver emerged. Maybe it was the fisherman I chatted with on the bridge. Maybe he had a stroke or a heart attack.

I plunged into the bay and swam to SUV. Its front end was submerged up to the windshield. I peered through the driver side window. A head was slumped over the steering wheel.

I grabbed for the door and yanked it open. An inert body slid toward me.

Paige Turner!

10

· · · · · · · · · · ·

When she came to, we were sitting next to each other in a booth at the Dynasty Diner on Main Street. I had my arm draped around her, supporting her. Her head languidly drooped on my shoulder.

"Where am I?" she asked.

"Well, you're not in Kansas anymore, Dorothy."

"How'd I get here?"

"You swam. Well, partially. I dragged you the rest of the way."

The diner owner appeared. A Greek man with a bald pate whose name was Mustafa. He was accompanied by a slender, olive-skinned, dark-haired hostess who had introduced herself as Sophia, his daughter.

She spoke first. "The EMTs are on their way. They should be here in about ten minutes."

"Can we get you anything?" the owner offered. "A bowl of soup?"

"A cup of tea would be nice," replied Paige. "Thank you."

"And for you, sir?"

I'd noticed their shelves behind the counter were stocked with wine and beer bottles.

"A Yuengling in a frosted mug." It wasn't my usual drink but at least it would be cold and contain alcohol. After the day I had, I needed both.

"Coming right up." When father and daughter went into action, I removed my arm from around Paige so that she could sit up. She was groggy. Her makeup was smeared but her Bare Essence was still intact. Even jostled and wet, she had a radiance I presumed matched her defiance.

"So, this is the reason you cancelled your flight to Kansas City yesterday," I said playfully. "To take a dip in Great Bay? Or was it just to run me down? Am I that irresistible?"

"Don't flatter yourself, Mac. I was tailing you."

"I hadn't noticed." I was cold and damp, hungry, and more than a little irritated, which can sometimes put me in a sarcastic mood. "Why? Do I owe you money? Did I break our date?"

"I'm an investigative journalist, Mac. That's what I do."

"Run people over?"

"I wasn't trying to run you over. I got lost. The Rogue is a rental. I couldn't figure out how to switch off the brights."

"Could have asked me. Where's your phone?"

Looking around for her pocketbook, Paige panicked.

"Where's my purse?"

"In the Rogue?"

"We have to go back. I need it. My phone, my wallet. I need them."

"How about your notes? And your sources. Names and addresses. If they're in there, too, I'll go with you. Otherwise, I'll wait until the Amos Brothers wrecker pulls it out of the drink. That's who our lovely hostess called when we arrived, and I told them what happened."

"That's not funny, Mac."

I was only half serious, but when I saw the concern register on her face at my mention of sources and notes, I knew I'd hit the mark.

"Relax, Paige," I said, putting my hand on hers. "Their shop is right next door. We can pick up your purse in the morning. And if the Rogue is dried out, you can return it to Enterprise."

"That means I'm staying here overnight?"

"You and me both."

"Together?"

"Honey, I've got a warm bed and a bottle of Jack waiting for me at the Surf City Hotel."

"And for me?"

"I imagine right now they're preparing a nice, safe, disinfected suite for you over at Southern Ocean County Medical Center."

"It's a nice hospital," agreed Sophia, setting down our drinks.

Paige took a dainty sip. I guzzled half the bottle, finishing with a commensurate belch. Under the circumstances I couldn't restrain myself.

Paige set down her cup. "So, I guess you saved my life, hey, Mac?"

"I certainly think you should ask for the money back on those swimming lessons your father paid for."

That was the first time I saw Paige Turner, Investigative Journalist, genuinely smile since I met her three days ago.

"You're funny, Mac."

"Is that why you were tailing me?"

"You know why I was tailing you."

"All the way from Trenton."

"All the way."

"What made you think I was on the case? A little birdy whisper in your ear?"

She greeted that comment with silence. I knew it couldn't be Shirley Mae or Mary. "Wait. I know you spoke to your editor." That was a stretch, because I pretended to be Chief Perkins when I spoke to Peters. He may have seen through the charade, but he couldn't have guessed it was some obscure PI from Trenton making that call.

"Let's just say it was a source."

"A confidential source?"

"All sources are confidential, Mac. You should know that. It's how we exist. It's called the First Amendment."

"It's how you avoid prosecution, you mean."

"It's how we protect sources who need to tell the truth without fear of revenge or reprisal."

"It's how someone with a perceived ax to grind can sound off without being called on it."

Paige yawned. It meant she'd had enough. Lord knows there was no right or wrong position for either of us. I was just feeling testy given the floor for an argument. I decided to change the subject while she was still awake.

"Why did you seek me out at Jake's?"

She yawned again, wider, deeper this time, just as the EMTs arrived, bearing a spotless stretcher. The tech gave her a shot to put her at ease even though she was already heading for la-la land on her own. She glanced at the stretcher. Then glanced up at me.

"To convince you to help me."

•••

Three hours later I was settled in my cozy little room at the Surf City Hotel on LBI, putting the cap back on the bottle of Old No. 7 half empty on my nightstand. I took a hot shower and felt renewed. It was a feeling I knew would fade as soon as my head hit the pillow.

My clothes were still damp, including my skivvies. They hung over the shower bar and towel racks. I never minded sleeping naked. I took an extra blanket from the closet and spread it over the bed.

I turned off the light and slid under the covers. They felt crisp and smelled clean. I fluffed up my two big down-filled pillows, putting one under my head and laying the other perpendicular beside me. For optimal sleep, I liked my pillows cold but my sheets warm. I rotated the pillows during the night.

I lay on my back with my hands under my head, thinking about the crazy events of the day. How strange life could be, I thought. In three days' time a strange but alluring professional woman walks into my life. I buy her a drink at my favorite bar and suddenly she's gone.

The next day I find out she's written a story accusing a friend of mine, who happens to be the top law enforcement officer of my fair city, of corruption. He, too, disappears. Then, while I go off searching for him in one of the most remote places in New Jersey, the strange and alluring professional woman who had left me high but not exactly dry at the bar so she could run her story, tries to run me off the road.

Instead, it is she who ends up under water, quite literally leaving me to fish her out. Her hero. And what do knights in shining armor who save damsels in distress get in twenty-first century America for their chivalry? An argument.

This was all too much for my tired mind to process. It was time to shut it all down. What I needed most was a good night's sleep to recharge my batteries. After a day like today there was no telling what would be in store for me tomorrow.

That was the last thought I had when I heard the knock on my hotel room door. It took me a minute to collect myself and remember where I was. Was I dreaming? No. The knock came again. More forceful this time.

I glanced at the clock on the nightstand: one-fifteen a.m. Who the hell could that be? "Go away. You have the wrong room," I shouted.

He knocked again. Persistence may be a virtue, but this was not the occasion for it. I stood, wrapped a bath towel around my naked body and headed for the door with a grimace on my face and a clenched fist ready to punch his lights out.

"What do you want?" I yelled upon opening the door.

My towel slipped from my grasp. Standing in the doorway under the dim hallway light was Paige Turner, looking fresh as a lily, dressed in her white hospital gown. Conveniently, she had it open in the front, tied ever so loosely. Under her arm was a bundle I presumed were her wet clothes.

I bent to retrieve my towel. "Leave it," she said, kicking it into the room.

"I couldn't sleep," she said naively as she untied her hospital gown. She let it drop to the floor leaving it in the hallway.

She pushed me gently back into the room. "Do you know how hard it is to get a taxi at this hour?" she said, stepping into the room and deftly closing the door behind her with her foot.

11

. . . .

Well, I can tell you I didn't need that extra blanket. Nor did I need to reach for my other pillow.

Sometime during the night, Paige must have gotten up and hung her wet clothes next to mine in the bathroom. Because she was in them now, and they were dry and slightly wrinkled.

Seeing her dressed and recalling the night before made my heart sink. "I'm guessing no round two this morning?" I said with a bit of whimsy.

"Are you kidding me, Mr. Marathon Man? I'm surprised you've got anything left!"

"I'm training for the decathlon," I managed to say while stretching. "I feel a burst of energy."

"Yeah, well, don't even think about an 'afternoon delight,' either. We've got a rental car to recover. And I could use a little breakfast. I need to refuel. I think you took some of that energy from my power station."

"It was worth it."

"I'm so glad I could please you, Mr. Cole. Now after you notch your belt, or bedpost or whatever, get your ass up and into the shower. I left you a towel."

"I use two. One for my body. One for my hair."

"Your body has hair. Use one."

I just loved a feisty woman in the morning, especially after a late night like we had had. It never ceases to amaze me how different a woman in a business suit can be when that business is pleasure. All a man has to do is get her to take off the suit.

...

The Rogue wasn't quite ready at the Amos Brothers Garage, so we ducked into the diner for some breakfast. The owner and his other daughter, Magdalena, greeted us warmly. Paige had French toast with fresh strawberries on top and two cups of Red Dragon tea. I had eggs Benedict to go with an endless pot of Greek coffee. It was dark and tasted like Ouzo. Or was that just my imagination?

Now that Paige had her purse back, she insisted on paying for breakfast. It was the least she could do, she said, for my having saved her life. I didn't dare tell her I'd already received all the reward I needed and then some. That might have set off another argument if she thought that I thought that she didn't get *some* enjoyment out of our lovemaking.

When the Amos Brothers returned her purse, she carefully checked its contents, even counting the cash to make sure everything was there. Apparently, nothing was missing. Then during breakfast, I noticed how she clung to the purse. It never left her side, even when she went to the loo.

Something of importance lay tucked inside that precious Burberry bag of hers. If I was a betting man, I would put money down that it was her story notes and source info. The source names and addresses might be on the phone, and since it's an iPhone I would imagine the Notes could be on there, too. No doubt both would be stored and encoded. Paige appeared to be the kind of woman who would guard personal information, hers and others'. That was both comforting and chilling. Chilling because it reminded me of how those blue eyes, when I first gazed upon them, signaled that no matter how pleasurable they were to behold – and, believe me, they are gem-like – some kind of secret lurked behind them. Perhaps multiple secrets that a woman in her profession would take with her to the grave.

Paige's iPhone had gotten wet inside the big bag. Not overly so, but the electronics were shaky. Magdalena suggested we seal the phone in a sandwich bag along with some uncooked rice. It was a trick she learned on the internet.

Watching Paige take her credit card out of her wallet made me think about her near-naked taxi ride at one a.m. How did she pay the fare? Naturally, the worst-case scenario popped into my depraved mind.

She somehow intuited my thoughts. "I take it you didn't look over your hotel bill very carefully this morning, did you, Mac? The night hotel clerk was very sympathetic and accommodating. I think he took pity on me."

"I didn't. I usually charge it and have the receipt sent to my secretary. She pays the bills."

"Well, prepare to explain how you could be in bed *and* in a taxi at one a.m."

Mary would spot something peculiar like that. She was a tenacious auditor in that sense. It was something she had picked from her prior employment at Axiom, where PYA was an essential way of life.

...

The news wasn't good when we walked back to the Amos Brothers Garage to pick up the Rogue. Salt water had seeped into the engine block and fuel line. It sputtered and coughed a lot. The techs did not recommend driving the car back to Trenton through the Pines. So, they called Enterprise, the rental car company, who sent a guy with another rental car to pick up Paige.

That left Paige fuming. She didn't want to wait around, and she certainly didn't want to get charged for another rental or for the damage to the one she took swimming. She would pay a $2,000 deductible, but because her newspaper was a national account, they would extend the rental agreement. But she had to accept a sub-compact Nissan Versa, as they had no more Rogues available.

Paige recounted the arrangements to me after she hung up the phone with the rental car clerk. She was still in a snit. She only got half of what she wanted – a free rental – but she still had to wait around the smelly garage a whole day, and that didn't appeal to her.

She looked at me with sad, puppy dog eyes and asked me what I had planned for the rest of the day.

"Going fishing," I replied as convincingly as I could.

She smiled coyly. "Want some company? I might bring you luck."

I had no doubt that Paige Turner did not know how to bait a fishhook, but she sure knew how to bait a man.

"You might get dirty and smell all fishy."

"I'm counting on it."

What can I say? Deep down, I'm a pig. A sucker, too. Or maybe I just can't refuse a woman in need. Although I despise a needy woman. There is a difference. One made you feel honorable. The other guilty.

Paige Turner was neither. She appeared strong, confident and self-reliant. Traits I wondered whether she picked up from her father. She was sexy, too. I knew that didn't come from him.

"Tell me about your father," I asked by way of conversation. We were in my car heading for the Tuckerton Seaport. I was stalling, trying to figure out how I could ditch my new traveling companion while I went in search of Bill Perkins. Taking her along with me was out of the question. But I had a sneaking suspicion her plan was to wait me out until I capitulated. No one could ever accuse Paige Turner of being a dummy. Just my luck, I had to consider her the enemy until I talked to Bill Perkins and found out what was really going on with these National Crime Bureau Reports.

"Did you ever read my dad's book, *Dark Mercy*?" she inquired.

No, but I had talked to him on the phone, the cantankerous old shit. "Yes," I lied, hoping that would be good enough for her.

"What did you think?" she pressed.

"Well, *The New York Times* didn't think much of it, so I guess my opinion doesn't really matter." There, that should cover it. Now let's change the subject.

"I never read it, either," she admitted to my surprise. "I mean, I started reading it when I was sixteen, but I couldn't get into it. My brother Penrose read it."

"Your twin brother, right?"

Paige jabbed my arm. "You been doing a little research on me? That's interesting. Should I be flattered or worried?"

"I was trying to find your phone number. You ran out of the bar so quickly we didn't have a chance to exchange numbers."

"Why would we want to exchange numbers? Did you think there was going to be a round two?"

"Well, no, but here we are."

"Yes, here we are. By the way, where are we going?"

"It's a beautiful day. Sunny, clear skies. Just taking in some fresh air and sun. After your little motor vehicle mishap yesterday, I thought this might do you some good."

"So, we're not going fishing?"

"Oops, I forgot my pole."

"You know how to use the one in your pants. Maybe it will work on fish, too."

Her audacious remark caught me off guard. I didn't expect it. I took my eyes of the road momentarily to see what her face would tell. Passive. No emotion at all. When I turned back, I was in the other lane. A tractor-trailer hauling huge jetty stones was barreling down on us. Paige screamed. The truck blew its horn repeatedly. I wrenched the car to the right, swerved and fishtailed up onto a sandy embankment. The truck roared by, narrowly missing us. The driver threw me the bird.

"I'm sorry," Paige whimpered. "I shouldn't have said what I said. I distracted you."

I was livid, my heart racing and head pounding. "Having you here is a distraction, Paige."

"Distraction, you mean like a pain in the ass?"

"What are you doing here? What am I doing here?"

"Looking for Bill Perkins, I would imagine. Same as me." Ah, the truth finally came out.

"Why? You've probably destroyed the man's career. What more do you want to do to him? What has he done to you?"

Silence.

"This isn't about beating out Topeka in *U.S. New and World Report*, is it?"

More silence.

"See. This is what I mean. Your so damn protective of your sources and your so-called professional ethics that I can't get a straight answer from you. In fact, can't get any answers."

I turned to face her. She was near tears. That would be a new look for her. One I'm not sure I wanted to see.

"The night at the bar, Mac. The night I ran into you there. That was not by accident."

"I know. Nick told me. You came to talk to the person who knew 'where all the bodies were buried.' Ha, ha, ha."

"No, Mac. I came to you because I wanted you to stop me from publishing that story."

12

. . . .

Before Paige could explain her latest bombshell remark, my cell phone buzzed. It was Mary. I should have checked in hours ago.

I turned to Paige. "I've got to take this."

"Do you want me to get out of the car?"

"No. I will."

"What will it take to have you trust me, Mac?"

"It's my secretary. She doesn't trust any woman I've slept with."

"Is that because she wants to sleep with you?"

"Have you seen my secretary?" I meant it to be flattering, but it didn't come out that way.

"Do I need to?"

I couldn't believe I was having this conversation with a woman I hardly knew. A professional woman who could say the raunchiest things, or nothing at all, when it suited her.

The phone chimed again. I jumped out of the car. Then reached back and removed the keys from the ignition. "Stay put."

Paige gave me an offended look.

"Hi, Mary," I said when I was out of earshot.

"Everything alright?"

"Yes, Mary. Everything's fine."

"I hate it when you say that, Mac. What's going on? Did you find Chief Perkins?"

I glanced back at the car. Paige was rummaging through my glove compartment. Cars blew by, making it difficult to hear Mary. I took another couple of steps into the woods.

"I haven't found him yet. Shirley Mae didn't give us much to go on."

"That's why I'm calling you. Shirley Mae didn't show up for her briefing this morning. Come to think of it, neither did you."

Mary sounded alarmed. I asked. "Has something happened to her?"

"That's just it. I don't know. But O'Malley just called looking for you."

"What did you tell him?"

"The truth. That you were out of town."

"What did he say to that?"

"You know O'Malley. At first, he didn't believe me. He got all huffy and tried to give me the third degree."

"He likes to throw his weight around. It's probably worse now that he's in charge."

Mary sighed. "Anyway, he said to have you call him."

"He didn't give you any idea what he wanted?"

"None."

"Do you think it has anything to do with Shirley Mae?"

"Hard to tell. But when I called TPD dispatch and asked to speak to her, they told me she wasn't in today."

"That's worrisome."

"I know."

There was a momentary pause in our conversation. The connection was still there, which can sometimes be erratic in the Pines. It was obvious wheels were turning. Mary spoke first.

"So, when can I expect you back in the office?"

"I don't know, Mary." I shot a quick glance over to Paige. She was out of the car fussing with her iPhone. She had it out of the bag, trying to get it to work while trying also to listen in on our conversation.

I took another step away. "I've got some unfinished business here."

"Does it have anything to do with the email receipt I got from the Surf City Hotel?"

"No. Why?"

"Why did you need to take a taxi to the hotel at one a.m.? Did something happen to your car?"

I swear that woman could smell female trouble on me from miles away.

"I'd been drinking," I lied.

"Mac, we've talked about this. You've got to slow down."

"I'm fine, Mary. Really."

I looked over at Paige. She was pacing around the car and looking none too happy.

"Say, Mary. It's noon. I don't expect to be back in Trenton anytime soon. Not until I find Bill, or at least talk to him."

"What are you saying, Mac?"

"Close the office. I don't want anyone calling. Cancel any appointments. Reschedule them for the end of week."

"And if I hear from O'Malley again?"

"Tell him the message was delivered. But close up shop before he does. He may come knocking. That's the kind of cop he is, when he wants to be. Real hound dog."

"Okay, Mac." She paused briefly. "Should I come back into the office tomorrow?"

I looked over at Paige. She was staring back at me icily. The daggers were out. Her patience was gone.

"Absolutely, Mary. I'll see you first thing in the morning."

"Even if you don't find Bill?"

"One way or another."

"Be careful, Mac. Wear a raincoat. It's supposed to rain today and tomorrow."

Good old Mary. Her instincts serve her well. A raincoat was code for a prophylactic. From my vague answers she suspected something was going on that may, or more likely not, have anything to do with the investigation. Something more personal.

"The weather's fine down here. You know what they say. LBI has its own weather. If you don't like it, wait a minute. It will change."

"That's what I'm afraid of, Mac." With that, she hung up.

Paige couldn't wait a moment longer. She was on me like a flea on a dog. Her hands all over me.

"I got bored," she said coyly. "Was the call really that important?"

"Just office stuff."

"TPD stuff?"

"Internal Affairs is still investigating."

"And you, Mr. Cole? Are you still investigating?"

"Listen, Paige. I don't know what kind of game you're playing, but I'm a straight shooter."

"So, let's go find Perkins and ask him."

"Ask him what?"

"To come clean. Tell us the truth. Aren't you curious?"

"Not like you."

"Listen, Mac. You may not know this, but I tried to see Perkins. That's why I came to Trenton. I wanted to hear his side. They told me he was unavailable. Then I tried to phone him. Same deal. That's why I canceled my flight back to Kansas."

"Gee whiz, and here I thought it was for me?"

"Not for you. Then I found out he skipped town. When I saw you leaving, too, I put two and two together."

"And here we are."

"Yes, here we are. Are you going to take me to Chief Perkins or not?"

"Honestly, I don't know where he is."

"Yes, you do. You're a PI, and a 'damn good one,' so I've been told."

"That's Nick talking. He likes to show off in front of the ladies."

"Yet I chose you over Nick. Why?"

"You need glasses? You like older men?"

"No silly. It's you I want. It's you I need to help with Perkins."

"For what? The damage has been done."

"If you believe that, than take me to him. We can make this right. Together. Exonerate him if that's where it leads."

"It was you who put him in this predicament to begin with."

"Yes, and I can get him out."

"How?"

"By telling his side of the story."

"What makes you suddenly think there is another side? Are you not confident in your half, the published story?"

"I am. But don't you find it strange that he's hiding out? What's he hiding from? That's why I need your help."

"Why does suddenly everyone need my help?"

"Because you have no agenda, Mac. Your aim is true. Your heart pure."

"Tell that to my ex-wife. Whoever told you that is full of shit."

"Then maybe you should fire your secretary."

"What?"

"Yeah, I screened you, too. Right after Nick dropped your name. Called your office. Pretended to be a potential client. Used a fake name, of course."

"You gave him *your* number."

"I gave him my father's old number. The disconnected one. As you discovered."

"Yes. I spoke to your father. Bet you get that defiant streak from him."

"Not really. I'm not like him at all. Dad has his protégé, Penrose. I didn't fit in. I guess I didn't have the right equipment."

"You and your dad are both writers. What does Penrose do?"

"He's a lawyer. Works in D.C. For the Justice Department."

"How is that working out?"

"I don't know. I haven't talked to him since the story broke."

My ringing cell phone startled me. I wasn't expecting any calls. The fact that it might be Mary with an update on O'Malley or Shirley Mae would be disconcerting. It was a number I didn't know.

The terse male voice on the other end of the line told me it was one of the Amos brothers. Paige's rental car replacement had arrived.

I was a bit put out by it. "You gave the Amos brothers my cell number."

"I don't have a working phone, remember."

I handed my phone to her. "It's for you. Your Vespa's here."

Apparently, she'd forgotten about it. Decision time. I knew this could be trouble. The situation had changed since this morning and was evolving still.

Arms folded, back braced for an argument, she gave me a stern look. "Tell them to take it back. I don't want it."

"How are you going to get back to Trenton?"

"I'll thumb it if I have to."

I damn well knew what that meant. As John Lennon said in a classic song, "I should have known better." Once they have sex with you, you're theirs. The only unknown was for how long.

13

· · · · · · · · · · · ·

The Tuckerton Seaport was a replica of an old-style fishing village, the type Tuckerton may have been at one time. Here visitors learned about the various trades and crafts of the old days: decoy duck carving, fish netting, fly tying, and the hematologic value of the horseshoe crab to modern medicine. Docents regaled visitors young and old with pirate tales of buried treasure and the ecological wonder of the bay teeming with life.

The sprawling complex was located on the lagoon just off Route 9. It also had a replica of the Tucker's Island Lighthouse, which once guided ships to safety along the shore, before it was swallowed by the sea back in the 1920s.

I didn't have a plan when we arrived at the Tuckerton Seaport just after noon. I was hoping Becky Gibson, the director who helped me the night before, might have some fresh ideas on where we could possibly try next to locate our elusive police chief.

The museum had about a half-dozen people milling about when we entered the gift shop, mostly seniors. Nautical scenes of ships and sea creatures decorated the walls. Becky was behind the counter talking with a silver-haired man in mechanic's overalls. She saw us and waved us over.

She greeted us cordially. "Well, hello, Mr. Cole. Back so soon? Is this the missing person you went searching for?" she added, apprizing Paige carefully. She knew it wasn't.

"Hi Becky. Not exactly." Truth was I was stumped on how to introduce Paige. I should have known she would take the lead and do it for me.

"Hi! I'm Paige Turner," she said, extending her hand with enthusiasm. "I'm working with Mac on this missing person case. Think of me as his associate."

"Assistant." I corrected.

"Whatever."

Becky blushed for both of us. "My, my, you two must be loads of fun out in the field together."

"You have no idea," Paige replied.

"Oh, and this is Bo Parker," Becky said, turning to the silver-haired man. He had the chafed and greasy hands of an auto mechanic. "He's the owner of Skinner's Marina, across the way. I was just telling him about our discussion regarding your mission to locate that certain person. I take it you were not successful."

Paige gave me a curious look. I think she found my methods here amusing. In the car on the way over I had purposely neglected to give Paige any details on what we were doing here. I wanted to give her as little context as possible. It was bad enough I couldn't shake her shadow. If she was really committed to learning Perkins' side of the story, this was her moment of truth.

"Afraid not, Becky. I drove up and down Great Bay Boulevard until I ran out of light. I saw plenty of houseboats, but none looked inhabited. Most looked like they'd seen better days. I'm certain the one I'm looking for would be well maintained. The man who owns it is fastidious and should be living there right now."

Paige nodded in agreement. "Neat as a pin and very demanding, he is."

I shot Paige a sharp glance. Don't overdo it.

"Well, maybe I can help," offered Parker. "What exactly are you looking for?

Becky jumped right in. "The tipster –" she looked over at me. "Can I use that term?"

I nodded.

"The tipster said it was a 'shack' located 'on the water.' So, that made me think of the houseboats down along Great Bay Boulevard. They are a bit run down, but since they sat 'on the water' I thought he should try there."

"They should tear 'em all down, if you ask me," Parker opined. "They're an eyesore and a haven for drug addicts and promiscuous teens."

"I agree," said Becky with an affirmative shake of her head.

"Wait," Parker exclaimed. "What was the other part?"

"'On. The. Water,'" I threw out, pronouncing each word separately and distinctly.

"You sure that's what you heard?"

"Quite sure."

"Round these parts, that's a euphemism for any place along the lagoon. Boaters consider that being *on the water* because of the easy access to the bay."

Becky concurred. "Now that you mention it, yes, I've heard it used that way."

"Where does that lead us?" I asked impatiently.

"Almost anywhere around the lagoon."

"Are there shacks on the lagoon?"

"Hardly. Most are moderately priced homes. For this area, that is. Maybe not what you're used to in Trenton."

I wouldn't be so sure.

"Hold on, now. Many of these people are acquaintances. I service their boats, sell them bait. This feller may be one of them. If he lives around here, around the lagoon, then, chances are he's been to my place. What does this man look like?"

"He's about six-two, maybe six-three. Two hundred twenty, twenty-five pounds," I said.

"Black as midnight," Paige added with emphasis.

Parker was taken aback. "Wait. A Black man, you say? Around these parts?"

"Yes," I concurred. I wanted to add "a civilized one," but that might have meant stepping farther into a conversation I wanted no part of.

Parker continued. "Ain't many. That's for sure. No work for them. Most work in the resort towns: Atlantic City, Somers Point, Cape May. Don't like the sun. Can't take the heat."

"So, he'd stick out like a sore thumb," Paige summarized perfectly.

"Yes, ma'am. He would. I believe I've seen this big feller. Comes to my shop to buy bait and gasoline. Matter of fact he was just there this morning. Drives a maroon Chevy Silverado. Has Jersey vanity plates. BIG 1 or something."

"That's him," I acknowledged. "How often does he come by?"

"Hard to say. Maybe once or twice a month. Sometimes I don't see him for weeks."

"That's because he lives in Trenton year-round. That's where his permanent home is," Paige provided.

"Thought so. Seemed odd to see him so sporadically."

"Do you know where he lives down here? Do you have an address?" I, too, was becoming excited, feeling the prospect that we might finally find him.

"On a receipt, maybe?" added Paige, thinking on her feet.

Parker shook his head slowly from side to side. "The man always pays cash. Like he'd been to the casinos in A.C. and won big."

"He's smart," Paige said. "He doesn't want you to know his business. He's a cop."

"Yeah, he does have that way about him."

"A commanding presence," I offered, to clarify everyone's thinking. "So, what you're saying is a Black man couldn't hide here if he wanted to."

"Yessir."

...

Clouds were forming overhead when we stepped from the gift shop back out into the parking lot. I wondered if they were an omen.

To speed things along, I enlisted Paige's help in putting the top up on the Jaguar. No point in getting a wet ass. When we'd finished, she asked, "So, what's the plan?"

"Lunch," I said without hesitation. I was starving.

We pulled onto Route 9 heading north and within two hundred yards made another turn into the parking lot of a Stewart's Root Beer. A teeny-bopper carhop came and took our order just as the rain gently began to fall on the canvas top we had put up just in time.

Paige, claiming she was still full from breakfast but probably trying to adhere to some kind of dietary restraint, ordered a bowl of lobster bisque and ice water with lemon.

I ordered two jumbo dogs with the works, fries, and a large root beer. As we waited for our food, listening to the rain, Paige again asked, "What's our plan for the day, Mac?"

I'd been thinking just that, ever since our conversation with the marina owner. To me it was a no-brainer. "For us, there is no plan. For me, after I drop you off at Amos Brothers Garage so you can commandeer your transportation back to Trenton, I'm off to continue looking for Bill Perkins."

"Ah, not fair," Paige protested. "I thought we were in this together."

"Has it ever occurred to you that maybe Bill Perkins doesn't want to see you?

Maybe that's why he's in hiding. He knows newshounds are relentless. You'll be a liability to me if I find him."

"I get it, Mac. You're right. Why would he want to talk to me? He's avoided me twice already. Why should I expect this time to be different?"

"In fact, it may be worse," I said. "The story's been published. You can't put the toothpaste back in the tube."

"No, but I can publish his rejoinder if there is one."

"I don't believe you *do* get it, Paige. Chief Perkins is a public official. His job revolves around having the public's trust. It will never be the same. There will always be that lingering doubt in the back of somebody's mind. The second-guessing about his motives. His naysayers and critics will have a field day. They'll be the first in line to resurrect the article and do the mudslinging."

"Yeah, I guess I do get that," she said with a sigh. "But I have to try. I have to do something."

"Let me ask you something. What did you mean when you said you sought me out to *stop* you from releasing the story? You also said something at the diner, when the

EMTs arrived, about wanting me to help you. Did you mean any of it, or were you just patronizing me?"

Paige turned her head and gazed out the window. The moment was punctuated by the arrival of our food. She lifted the lid to her soup cup and poked at it with her plastic spoon. I launched into one of the jumbo dogs, paid for our meals, and sputtered "thank you" to the young carhop.

Paige stopped playing with her soup. She watched me gorge myself, amused, I imagined, and then she spoke.

"I can understand why you don't trust me, Mac. Our intimacy last night, as wonderful as it was, doesn't absolve me of all my sins. So let me throw something out on the table that might tilt the scales in my direction a little."

My turn to be silent. Besides, my mouth was full. I finished one dog, slurped down some soda, fingered a few fries, and said, "Nothing short of revealing your sources will convince me to trust you, Paige. That way I'll know you're on the level, and I'll have a better understanding of where this whole thing got its start."

"You're still thinking it's a smear campaign."

"Yes, unless you or Perkins can convince me otherwise."

I bit into the remaining dog. Paige pointed to her mouth, indicating I had some mustard clinging to my moustache. I swiped at it with my napkin. She ate a spoonful of soup as the rain came down harder, fogging the windshield and obscuring our view. The confinement felt a bit eerie to me, and uncomfortable, even for two people who had recently been intimate. We were still strangers.

"Do you remember me asking you about my dad's book, *Dark Mercy*?"

"The one you didn't read?"

"That's right. But you did. What was it about?"

Moment of truth. I felt suddenly embarrassed. Caught lying for the sake of lying. Okay, I admit I was trying to impress Paige Turner back then. Looks like it backfired.

"Actually, Paige, I never read it either."

"You mean you lied to me?"

"Not exactly. I read the CliffsNotes version."

"What does that mean *exactly*?"

"The summary on Wikipedia."

"Hmm. So, you don't know anything about it?"

"Not really. Why? Is it important?"

"I'm not sure. But I believe the book holds the key to everything."

"How do you know, if you've never read it? From what I recall, it's a novel about a race discrimination incident that takes place somewhere in New York. Apparently, the perpetrators walk away scot-free. I don't see how that connects to Trenton."

"Neither do I, but my sources do, and I have faith in my sources."

"Here we go again with your precious sources. Why do you protect them so?"

Paige paused, sighing deeply. "Because, you idiot, one of my sources is the book's author."

"Your father?"

"And another is my brother, Penrose."

"Does Peters know this?"

"Yes, I'm sure he does."

"So, what's their angle, these sources?"

"It's me, I'm guessing. I've got the access to the press. That's why I'm a little hesitant now that I went with the story without doing my usual due diligence. I trusted the sources. Of course, the *U.S. News and World Report* graph with the data from the National Crime Bureau backed it up."

New revelations. This information was stunning. Finally, something to go on. Now we were getting somewhere. It could be a game changer. It felt like the ice dam just broke open. It explained a lot but not all. Paige really *was* trying to come clean, albeit after the fact.

I started the car. "Let's go." I barked, honking the horn and pushing our tray out the window for the carhop to take away. She sloshed through the rain to take it before I sped off. I rolled up the window.

"Where are we going?"

"To the Tuckerton Library to get a copy of *Dark Mercy*."

"It's out of print."

"Then we'll try Amazon or eBay. There must be a copy out there somewhere. Did you bring a laptop?"

"No. I left it at the hotel in Trenton. You?"

"I don't use one. In the office I use a clumsy old desktop model with a tower, or I have Mary use hers."

"Why don't you just have Mary order it online?"

"I sent her home for the day. Besides I'm down here. I need it now."

"What do you hope to find after you've read it?"

"The same thing you're after. What every good investigative journalist and PI worth their salt should be after. The truth!"

14

. . . .

The Tuckerton Library was a bust. They didn't have a copy of *Dark Mercy*.

Neither did the Barnes and Noble in the shopping plaza or any of the local independents that we called with the assistance of a kindhearted, underappreciated librarian named Agnes Moony. Paige was about to try the library's online resource center computer when my cell phone rang. Another unknown caller. But this one didn't need an introduction.

"Cole, I know where you are and what you're up to."

"O'Malley, how did you get this number?"

"You're not the only one who can be persuasive when it comes to the ladies."

I glanced at Paige. She was listening. Evidently, she recognized O'Malley's name.

"What do you want?"

"A chat. I'm here at your hotel in Surf City."

"It's a lovely place. The staff is very accommodating. I highly recommended it."

"Cut the crap, Cole. I could have you arrested for interfering in police business."

"You mean doing your job again, don't you?"

"The IA boys have it all under control. I've got Shirley Mae with me. I know about your little scam."

Scam is hardly the word I would use for shadowing law enforcement in a case involving one of their own. Then panic began to creep in when I realized Shirley Mae was the only one who could lead us to Chief Perkins, a man who apparently didn't want to see any of us. Now that circle was broadening. It included O'Malley, who could be a hardass. He would find a way to throw the book at me.

I was sure O'Malley wasn't bluffing but I needed to know Shirley Mae was okay.

"Put Shirley Mae on. I want to hear her voice."

"You think I'm bluffing? She's a cop, Cole. She works for me, not you. I think she's learned that lesson. And I don't take orders from you."

"Put her on, O'Malley, or I'll make sure Perkins fires your ass when I bring him back to headquarters and he kicks you out of his office."

"Now who's bluffing?"

At the moment, O'Malley seemed to hold all the cards. Without Perkins, I had nothing.

"Alright, Alright. Stay put. I'm on my way."

For a sleepy little fishing town, Tuckerton was suddenly getting a bit crowded with surly visitors. No doubt the excitement would be dizzying to residents like Becky Gibson, Bo Parker, and Agnes Moony – and more than a little comical.

I told Agnes the librarian we had to run and thanked her for her help. I needed to use the restroom. Paige took the opportunity to do the same. No telling when the chance might come again.

While washing up I felt the vibration of a text message alert. Inept at using my thumbs on those tiny keyboards, I rarely sent texts and thus rarely received any. I dried my paws under the deafening Air Blade, pulled out the phone and read: "I hear you're looking for me. If you want to talk, come now. 13 Pinecone Lane. Come alone!"

I recognized the number. Bill Perkins.

Ditching my new traveling companion was not going to be easy. Since our roll in the hay, we were practically joined at the hip like a joyous couple. A couple of what? I didn't really know, but it was time to shake loose.

We bumped into each other exiting the restrooms. It was an awkward moment that led to a more awkward moment when I told Paige I needed her to stay and finish researching *Dark Mercy* online while the library remained open.

"Where are *you* going?" she inquired.

"I'm going to face O'Malley alone. There's no telling how he will react with you in tow. It's too risky. He's liable to arrest us both on the spot."

"He can do that?"

"Believe me. He's that kind of cop. You know the good cop/ bad cop scenario you see on TV? O'Malley is the bad cop every time. He's not role playing."

"How long you think you'll be gone?"

"As long as it takes to get O'Malley off our backs."

"You're not ditching me, are you, Mac?"

"Not a chance, sweetheart. I'll be back. I promise." I gave her a tender peck on the cheek for reassurance and dashed out the door before she could put up a stronger protest. Bogie would have been proud.

•••

Twelve minutes later my GPS had me parking in front of 13 Pinecone Lane. It was on the eastern edge of the lagoon and the only dwelling on the street. Two lots were vacant. A small boat was tied to the bulkhead behind a single-story frame house with dated mauve fiberglass siding. The marina owner was right. This was no shack, but no palace, either.

Perkins' maroon Chevy Silverado was backed in over the pea stone gravel in front of the house. Chief Perkins, in a tan tee shirt and blue jeans, was dangling over the side of the boat with a paint brush, varnishing the keel haul. He put the brush down and stood up on the deck when he saw me approach.

"Permission to come aboard?" I said, stepping onto the pier.

"Permission granted," he replied. He offered his hand and pulled me across the gangplank. Then he reached into a cooler and pulled out two bottles of Michelob.

"Now you're talking," I said gratefully, taking the cold beer.

He sat in his captain's chair, leaning it back and tilting it toward me. I sat on a foam cushion atop the bait box.

"Shirley Mae referred to this place as a shack," I said by way of an opening. "It's anything but."

"She called it the 'love shack,'" he added with a chuckle. "That explains how you found me. My wife loved it, too. That's why I kept the tax records under her name, Edith Bailey, as I'm sure you were wondering."

"I was, and, actually Bill, you found me. How did you know I was looking for you?"

"I forgot the varnish. Had to go back to Skinner's this afternoon. The owner told me he ran into you."

"I guess good news travels fast."

"In these parts, nothin' moves fast. That's why I come down here. To chill."

"Sorry I interrupted."

"If not you, would have been somebody else. Why'dja bring the bitch reporter along?"

"Everybody's looking for you, Bill. O'Malley's on LBI as we speak. He's got Shirley Mae and, I'm sure, an army of IA boys with him."

"O'Malley couldn't fight his way out of a wet paper bag. He needs an army."

"Is that why you left him in charge?"

"I had my reasons."

"Knowing you, I'm sure you did. Still, everyone wants to know why you disappeared."

"I'm on administrative leave. I can go where I please."

"Sure you can. But you left a hell of a mess behind."

"It was necessary."

"I don't doubt it, but your silence complicates things. You didn't even try to defend yourself – or the squad. They're feeling abandoned."

"So, they hired you?"

"Luck of the draw, I guess. They want to know why you haven't come out with a statement giving your side of things."

"Is that what the bitch is after?"

"That's what she says. Says she tried to contact you before she went to press. Said you refused to see or even talk to her."

"She's got that right."

"Help me understand your side, Bill."

"No need to worry, Mac. It'll all shake out in the end."

"I don't get it. Did you deep-six those serious crime reports in 2020 to make the department look good or not?"

"Is that what you think?

"That's what a lot of people think because of your silence and sudden disappearance."

"I know what they think, Mac. My reputation's been tarnished. I got a black eye in this fight. But I ain't been knocked down, and I certainly ain't been knocked out. We're in the early rounds of this. Their day will come."

"You say that like somebody's out to get you. Is somebody trying to smear your reputation? Do you know who it is?"

"I can't prove anything. But I smell a rat."

"Is it O'Malley? Everyone knows he wanted your job."

"I ain't saying nothing, Mac."

"What, you're just gonna leave it up to Internal Affairs to sort out? O'Malley already seems to have cozied up to those boys. I wouldn't put it past him to throw Shirley Mae under the bus and make her the scapegoat. And you're gonna sit here and do nothing."

"I'm doing something. I'm following the best advice anyone ever gave me. He told me that when he worked at Axiom, he had a boss he admired greatly. He told me that boss's best decisions were made when he did nothing at all. He just sat back and let the chips fall where they may. Now finish your beer and git."

I stood and downed the bottle in three gulps. I couldn't argue with a man who used my own words as his defense. That boss had another piece of advice: "Kill your own skunks." I neglected to pass that one on to Chief Perkins. I was wondering now if it also applied to rats."

"I've got one more question for you."

"Shoot."

"Does the novel *Dark Mercy* mean anything to you?"

"Not a thing."

...

"You saw him, didn't you? You saw Perkins. I knew you couldn't be trusted. After what I divulged to you. Oh, I feel like such a fool."

We were in my car heading for LBI to rescue Shirley Mae. The rain had stopped. A bit of sun was peeking through the clouds.

O'Malley had called twice during my chat with Chief Perkins. Each message he left got nastier and more expletive-laden.

"Relax, Paige. Perkins made it clear that he would not see me if you came along. I had no choice."

"So, what did he say?"

"Nothing."

"Yeah, right."

Lying to Paige Turner didn't win me any favors before, so I figured maybe I should stick to the truth from now on. Anyway, the truth came easier to say. No guilt attached. No worry of being found out. But the truth was harder to discern when you didn't possess all the facts.

"Did you ask him if he doctored those records?"

"Point blank. Yes."

"And?"

"He neither confirmed nor denied it."

"What does that mean?"

"Honestly, I don't know. But I do know you would have gotten the same answer from him if you were there. And when I asked him about *Dark Mercy*, he said he didn't know anything about it."

"And you believe him?"

"Frankly, I don't know what to believe. But I'm hoping O'Malley can steer us in the right direction."

"O'Malley? What's he got to do with this?"

As I said, lying was one vice I swore off, but telling Paige everything I knew, everything Perkins and I talked about, was another kettle of fish. Safer to keep my suspicions about O'Malley's involvement under the radar until I had proof. I got the sense that's how Perkins was playing it. So, damn it, so was I.

15

· · · · · · · · · · ·

I expected to find Shirley Mae hogtied with a sock in her mouth. But that would have been giving O'Malley too much credit.

Paige, for her part, decided she still wanted to come along. Somehow, I just knew that would be trouble. Explaining her to O'Malley, after the way she had scandalized the TPD, was sure to throw the detective over the edge. I looked forward to it.

I found O'Malley chain-smoking and pacing the sidewalk outside the hotel. He had on a rumpled trench coat, and his receding dark hair was matted by the rain. The temporary promotion to Interim Chief had not improved his appearance. Beside him, two uniformed Internal Affairs officers stood erect. Shirley Mae Brown sat in a white Adirondack chair, her face downcast.

"'Bout time, Cole," he bellowed. "What took you so long?"

I decided not to lie to O'Malley. Well maybe just white lies. "I had a long chat with Chief Perkins."

"Did you, now?" He glanced around. "Where is he?"

"Let's just say he's at an undisclosed location, plotting his return."

"Is that supposed to be some kind of threat?"

"Take it as you will."

He studied Paige, undressing her with his eyes. "Who's the babe?"

"My new assistant." White lies do come in handy sometimes.

"Yeah, right. And I'm the tooth fairy."

Paige stepped forward. There was no holding her back. "I'm Paige Turner, the investigative journalist who wrote the *Sun Times* article that was picked up by the AP." She didn't extend her hand.

The two IA boys stiffened. O'Malley tossed his cigarette on the ground and stepped on it.

"You're the reporter who blew the whistle on Perkins."

"We don't know the full extent of the data aberration, but if that offends you, I apologize. I'm paid to print the truth."

"So you say."

"Maybe you should thank her, O'Malley." I was feeling testy, hoping to get a reaction out of him I could gauge properly. "She's the reason you finally get to sit in the chief's chair. Although I wouldn't get too comfortable. It is only temporary."

Shirley Mae lifted her beleaguered head. "Did you really see the chief, Mac? Is he alright?"

"Yes, Shirley Mae. He expressed his concern for you. Are *you* okay?"

"I'm fine – just disappointed I let you and him down."

"On the contrary. There's a light at the end of the tunnel."

"Whaddya mean?"

"Perkins has a plan. Just you hang in there."

"A plan for what?" O'Malley questioned sharply. "It's in IA's hands. Perkins has no say in the matter. He's the one under the microscope, here."

"That's not the way he sees it."

Paige shot me a dirty look. I could read her face. She thought I'd lied to her again, that Perkins had confided in me his side of the story. He hadn't. But that's exactly what I wanted O'Malley to believe.

"The guilty never do see it any other way but their own," said O'Malley, lighting another cigarette.

"He'll have his hearing."

O'Malley glanced at the two guards. "We're all looking forward to it," he snickered.

"What do you plan to do with Shirley Mae?" I inquired discreetly, although I already knew. Someone has to go down. It was O'Malley's way of showing he was in charge.

"She'll have her hearing, too, where she'll be charged with insubordination, and more, if Internal Affairs finds she's been complicit in this data rigging affair with Perkins."

"You're assuming an awful lot of O'Malley. Like you always do."

"The facts don't lie, Cole. Just ask your reporter friend."

He looked at Paige. "Ain't that right, honey?"

"If that's how the investigation turns out, yes."

He turned back to confront me. "As for you, Cole, I recommend you drop what you're doing and go back to Trenton. I'm sure your inbox is stuffed with better things to do. We can handle our own affairs. And take the lady reporter with you. She's done enough damage to the department."

While the cat's away, the rats will play. No way was I going to let O'Malley run roughshod over the Trenton Police Department even if Chief Perkins himself was willing to let it happen, temporarily!

"I'll make you a deal, O'Malley, I'll quit poking this hornet's nest, provided you cut Shirley Mae some slack.

She's a dedicated, tenured employee whose family depends on her. She's covered for your ass on many occasions. You owe her. Her only sin in this whole affair was her loyalty to the chief."

"Wrong, Cole. Her mistake was taking a police matter outside the force. Her sin was taking it to you. For that, she has to pay."

"Mercy is a virtue, O'Malley, haven't you heard?" I glanced at Paige and then at Shirley Mae. "I implore you, as interim chief, to exercise sound judgment and show some mercy here."

"I have no idea what the hell you're talking about, Cole. The answer is no. Now get out of my sight." He tossed his cigarette into the street. To the officers, he barked, "Grab her and let's go."

...

Paige said, "You came down really hard on O'Malley today."

We were eating dinner at the Surf City Hotel, having just re-reserved my room from the previous night for a second tryst. This time I came clean and told them it would be for two guests. In the last twenty-four hours I'd become so honest I was beginning to feel like a damn Boy Scout.

The Surf City Hotel was the "in" spot during the season. Newly acquired and renovated by young owners, the hotel boasted three bars plus spacious indoor and outdoor patio dining. It's where Nick Falcone got his start as a bartender while on hiatus from performing in summer stock shows at the Surflight Theatre.

Open all year, the hotel's executive chef had trained in some of the finest restaurants in Europe and America.

Going light, Paige was enjoying her grilled branzino with sauteed string beans and garlic potatoes. I went with the Caesar salad and house specialty, short ribs in ginger Thai sauce. Forsaking our normal cocktails, each of us was on our second vodka martini.

"He deserves it," I said, not holding back.

"You don't like him, do you?"

"Everybody on the force tolerates him, but I don't have to."

"What's his problem, anyway? Besides being an egotistical, pompous ass, I mean."

"He's reckless. He makes assumptions, draws conclusions about cases, always thinking he's got it right. No one else's opinion matters."

"I can see that."

"This situation is a good example. You heard him. He's so damn sure that Perkins orchestrated the omission of the TPD serious crime records that he's ready to string him up. Facts aren't always clear and substantial. They can point to several conclusions. But not to O'Malley. His mind is made up."

"Is that it?"

"He harbors racial prejudice, which is not an asset for a cop in a city like Trenton."

"I noticed you dropped the mention of 'mercy' into the conversation with O'Malley. Was that calculated?"

"I'm looking for answers, Paige. You saw his reaction. It's the same one I got from Perkins. Are you sure there is a connection between the book and the Trenton Police Department?"

"No. That's what I've been trying to tell you. I overheard my father and brother talking about it after dinner several weeks ago. I wasn't paying much attention to the conversation because I had work to do.

"The next day, my father shows me the *U.S. News and World Report* article. He plants the idea in my head of a possible story involving police corruption perpetrated by underreporting their statistics in order to mislead the public and make law enforcement in the city look good. He suggested I pitch the idea to Peters, my editor, but failed to tell me he already had. Peters loved the idea of rocking the sociopolitical boat in an urban northeastern sanctuary city like the one in *Dark Mercy*. Now where did he get that idea from?

"So, I asked him. He said it was just an inside joke between him and my dad. That I should only concern myself with writing the story. Meanwhile Peters did all the fact-checking and obtained the required legal verifications from the magazine staff and the Justice Department. All I had to do was write the story."

"You never spoke to any other sources?"

"No. And neither did Peters, that I know of. I tried to get Perkins on the record. That's why I flew to Trenton. But on the flight, I got to thinking something wasn't quite right. About how the story came about. That's what I was hoping Perkins could sort out for me."

"Because it started with your father and brother following their discussion of his novel *Dark Mercy*."

"Exactly. When I couldn't get in touch with Perkins, I figured, 'Let me go find someone local who I'm told has his finger on the pulse of crime in Trenton.'"

"That would be me."

"So I was told."

Dessert arrived in the form of a parfait, which we shared. Afterward we procured a bottle of prosecco and took it back to the room.

16

· · · · · · · · · · ·

I don't remember finishing the prosecco, but I woke up naked around three a.m. with a bit of a headache. Paige was lying next to me, also naked, sound asleep.

I got up to relieve first my bladder, then my head pain. Though I never carried it when I traveled, as some people do, acetaminophen was my drug of choice at times like this but, because of its repudiated effect on the liver, I limited my usage. I was already doing enough damage to it in other ways.

After glancing in the bare medicine cabinet, I spied Paige's Burberry bag on the bedroom chair. Paige, because of her job, mentioned the night we met at Jake's that she traveled a lot. She struck me as the well-prepared type who would carry emergency supplies with her. She had the right bag for it.

Lifting the Burberry, noting its heft, I crept into the bathroom so I would not disturb Sleeping Beauty. I shut the door and switched on the light.

I plugged the sink drain, unzipped the bag, held it upside down, and deposited its contents into the sink. Everything imaginable came tumbling out: comb, wallet, brush, nail file, condoms, compact, iPhone (in baggie with rice), notebook, pens, various prescription bottles and – bingo! – extra-strength Tylenol. What I didn't expect was the dogeared paperback copy of *Dark Mercy*!

No wonder she never let her bag out of her sight. How we rushed to retrieve it from the rental car. She had it with her the entire time we called around to bookstores and stopped in the library. All along the book was tucked in her bag, as well as the rest of her secrets.

The bathroom door swung open. Paige, naked and yawning, stepped into the light. She saw me holding her empty bag over the sink. At first she looked shocked and furious; then she said, "I can explain."

"You'd better! And quick!" I was more embarrassed than pissed. I had let my guard down and trusted her. *I should have known better.* There was that Beatles song again!

"Don't be mad, Mac. Hear me out."

"You lied to me, Paige. You said you never read the book. It looks thoroughly read to me."

"I didn't read it. I swear. What I told you was the truth. I tried to read it when I was sixteen but couldn't get through it."

"Uh huh."

"What I told you at dinner was also true. Suddenly, this book somehow played a role in the story I was writing, and I didn't know why."

"I'm listening." God, she looked great naked. It had to be the hot yoga. The rest was natural. The good Lord sure knew what he was doing when he pulled that rib from Adam's side. What Adam got in return for a lousy rib was a real bargain. In spite of myself, it was hard to focus on the story, if you catch my drift.

"So, I took the copy that was in my brother's room to read on the flight over. I didn't finish it until today after you dumped me at the library and went to see Chief Perkins without me."

"You finished it?"

"Yes."

"You want to give me the abridged version, or would you prefer I stay up all night and read it myself?"

"I'd prefer you come back to bed. I'll tell you there. Just please let me pee first."

Respectfully I put her things back in her handbag and went back to bed to wait for her. She took an extraordinarily long time, no doubt touching up her hair and gargling with cold water before she shut off the light and slipped back into bed. Her warm body was smooth as butter. We needed to move this story along or something unexpected might come up!

She placed her hand on my groin and smiled. "I'll be brief. I see your mind is elsewhere."

Men are so obvious.

"So, what did we learn? What's the story about?"

"The story is set in 1993 and takes place in the fictional town of Fulton, New York, located somewhere in the Bronx along the East River, in a context of mounting racial tensions and social problems as the growing ethnic population competes with the 'native' white population for limited jobs. Three Black teens – boys, really – are accused of fatally stabbing a homeless veteran while allegedly attempting to steal his drugs. First to arrive on the scene are a rookie cop and his partner.

"The murder weapon is found, and it supposedly has one of the boys' fingerprints on it. But the cop thinks his partner may have planted the knife. As the case comes up for trial, the weapon is reexamined, and it's found to be clean – the prints are gone. Some members of the Black community are up in arms, saying there never was any fingerprint evidence tying the knife to the boys. Without hard evidence, the prosecution drops the charges, and the three teens walk free. Can you see why a sixteen-year-old girl had a hard time getting into this story?"

"I'm surprised a thirty-seven-year-old woman could."

"Hey, no fair guessing. Anyhow, the story has a happy ending. The three teens go on to lead productive lives and become pillars of the community. One even becomes a cop. Meanwhile, the rookie cop agrees to drop the accusation against his partner and transfers to another precinct with a commendation."

"Where did your father come up with the story idea?"

"I asked my brother once, and he told me Dad based it on a real incident that happened in Poughkeepsie. He didn't know anything more than that."

"I don't get it. I don't see how it ties into Trenton, or this situation, at all."

"That's what's so confusing. Dad writes the book. It doesn't sell. Thirty years later, the story comes up in a family conversation in connection with an unrelated data scam, my editor jumps on it, passes it to me, and bam! It's published."

"It's like something has come full circle. But I don't know what."

"It does feel that way, doesn't it?"

Poor Paige. The story nearly put me to sleep. I was yawning and flaccid and having trouble keeping my eyes open. But I was warm.

"So, where do we go from here?" she asked, resting her head on my chest.

"To sleep, unless you've got a better bedtime story. One that will keep me... up."

17

. . . .

I waited in the dining room for Paige to join me following her morning meditation and tai chi practice. I was surprised she had any energy left. I sure didn't. But then I recalled my first impression that she worked hard at keeping herself attractive and fit. Therein lay the difference between the two of us. I worked hard at doing the complete opposite.

The breakfast buffet at the Surf City Hotel was an impressive hot and cold spread, but neither of us had much of an appetite. We sat in a moody silence.

"So, is this the end of the line for us, Mac?" Paige asked, breaking the reverie. She set down her empty teacup with a clatter clearly intended to rouse me from my musings. It did. But it took me a minute or two to process what she was asking.

I stared at her, unblinking. "There was no beginning. As I recall, you crawled into my bed two nights ago uninvited."

"Oh, that's cruel, Mac. I noticed you didn't throw me out."

"What can I say? I was cold."

I gave her a big, boyish "just kidding" grin. When she realized I was joking, we both started to laugh like two kids sharing a secret. In the last two days, we shared something real special. But was it over? That question was two-pronged – the personal and the professional – and at least one of the prongs I was not prepared to answer.

Paige probed further. "Seriously Mac, where do we go from here?"

"We go back to the office. We get Mary to reserve you a seat on the next available flight back to Kansas City while I try to figure out if I've got any moves left to save Perkins from going down in flames. A lot depends on whether Perkins chooses to make a public statement before his hearing."

"I'd like to stay around for the hearing," she said coyly, perhaps looking for encouragement from me. When I gave her none, she asked, "Do you know when the hearing will be?"

"Any time, now, I would expect. O'Malley appeared pretty confident. I don't imagine there were many records to go through in 2020. Or people to interview. Seems pretty clearcut. Chief Perkins was the one charged with authorizing the records. It's his signature that goes on each report. He either sent them in or he didn't. If he says he sent them, then where are they?"

"Sounds like a done deal."

"Right. Except for a couple things that don't add up. What Shirley Mae said about the records. She's sure some are missing."

"That doesn't bode well for Perkins."

"Agreed. But he has faith in the system that something will shake out."

"What's the other?"

"O'Malley. He's involved somehow, or Perkins would not have left him in charge. I sense Perkins thinks O'Malley knows something and is going to have to come clean. So Perkins is giving him enough rope to hang himself or to help exonerate him. That's the only sensible explanation I can come up with."

"You think Perkins believes O'Malley tossed the 'TPD serious crime' records. But how, if Perkins signed off on them when they were sent?"

"That's the big mystery. That's the piece of the puzzle I can't seem to put in place. Would O'Malley stoop that low to oust Perkins? Probably if the opportunity arose, but I don't think he'd go looking for it. O'Malley can be lazy, like I said. But how did he pull it off?"

"O'Malley has the motive," Paige concurred. "He has no great affection for Perkins, as you've pointed out, or loyalty to the force. From his vantage point, it would certainly be nice to retire in a couple years with a pension padded by the additional pay and standing of chief, even if not fully earned."

These thoughts, and the wild wind blowing in our hair and across our faces, limited the conversation as we drove northwest in the early morning sunshine back toward Trenton with the top down on the Jaguar. Outside of town, I stopped for gas and asked Paige if she wanted to go straight to the airport. She declined.

Mary greeted us with a warm hug for me and an icy stare for Paige Turner, after a brief introduction. Mary quickly recovered and told me I had a visitor waiting.

"Shirley Mae's in your office. She's been fired. O'Malley gave her the ax. She's absolutely beside herself with anger and fear. I told her on the phone you weren't back yet. She insisted on coming here and waiting for you. I didn't know what else to do."

"It's fine, Mary. You did the right thing."

I motioned to Paige to follow me into the office. "I want you to hear this. You may get that story you were looking for yet."

Mary sat back down behind her desk. She looked displeased but said nothing.

Stepping into the back office, Shirley nearly bowled me over. Her head came to rest on my chest. She then gave me her patented bear hug, just about squeezing the life out of me.

"What's she doing here?" she said, with ill tidings toward Paige.

"She's here to write your story, Shirley Mae Brown."

"Won't need to, if you brought Chief Perkins back with you."

"The chief is doing his own thing."

"Do he know what happened to me?"

"I don't think so, Shirley Mae."

"You gots to tell him, Mac. He need to know."

"Tell me exactly what happened with O'Malley."

"When we came back to Trenton yesterday after we seen ya'll, he told me to pack my things and clear out. Can you imagine? After thirteen years of dedication?"

"What about the IA boys? Did he clear it with them?"

"Said he didn't have to. Said it was a simple matter of insubordination."

Right. The only thing simple about it was Greg O'Malley. "Did IA interview you? Did you give them a statement?"

"Didn't get around to it. I was pulling records the first two days, then hustled down to LBI with O'Malley after he caught me reviewing the records and making my notes to report to you. Then he fired me."

"Do you still have your notes?"

"No. He took 'em and threw 'em in the trash."

"Can you remember what you wrote down?"

"Is the pope Catholic? Every word."

"Let's hear it. Wait! Let me get Mary in here."

"I can do that, Mac," Paige volunteered, pulling her notepad and pen from her bag. She took a seat opposite Shirley.

"Begin."

Shirley looked directly at Paige as she spoke. "You know I've worked here thirteen years. Chief Perkins hisself hired me. I done many jobs but now just mostly handle the dispatch lines. I was here in 2020. I answered and routed my fair share of the calls. Some involving very serious crimes where people were killed. I don't know how many were outright murders or what the wind-up was in court on all of them, coz it ain't my job to know. Except for one. Estelle Jenkins. A Black woman. Age 40. She was killed in a drive-by shooting back in 2020."

"And how come you remember that one?" asked Paige, settling into her reporter habit.

"She was my neighbor."

Shirley stopped, recalling the still-painful memory, then glanced my way for encouragement.

"Go on," I urged.

"The police believed the shooting was intended for Estelle's drug-lord boyfriend. He was one bad dude. But it never got solved. They never found out who did it.

"I also remember coz early 2021 I sent the 2020 reports to the National Crime Bureau. Back then it was one of my jobs. I remember holding Estelle's report in my hand and getting misty all over again. She was my close friend."

"Then what did you do?" asked Paige.

"I entered it into the computer like I did all the rest."

"You're sure?" I challenged. "All of them."

"Yessir. Every last one."

Paige studied the overweight dispatcher with a look of sympathy and concern. "Is that it?"

"No. In April 2021 we received a letter from someone in the Justice Department, a lawyer, saying the data we sent had gotten corrupted in the transmission. They said it was unreadable and that we needed to resend it."

I stopped her there and asked, "How is it you recall that so specifically, Shirley Mae?"

Silence.

I prodded. "Shirley Mae?"

"Because the chief was on vacation, fishing at his place in Tuckerton. He said the stripers were running. He didn't want to miss it."

Paige swiveled in her seat to face Shirley Mae directly. "Are you quite certain of the timing?"

"I am. Yes."

"And how are you so certain of the time and activities of Chief Perkins? Was it one of your jobs to maintain his schedule?"

Shirley shot me a glance. I had a hunch what was coming and knew I shouldn't stop her. The only remaining question was, could Paige be trusted with the information?"

"Go on, Shirley Mae," I said. "You're gonna have to tell the investigators at some point if you really want to help the chief."

"I was supposed to go with him. But one of my babies got sick."

If Paige was in shock by the revelation, she didn't show it. Instead, she instinctively reached out her hand and took

Shirley Mae's in hers. Never underestimate the solidarity of womanhood when trouble comes calling.

"What happened next, Shirley Mae?" I asked. "With the chief away, whose responsibility was it to respond to the Justice Department's request?"

She replied without hesitation. "The Chief of Detectives, Gregory O'Malley."

"Ah, now we're getting somewhere. And did he send them?"

"No sir. I did."

"You? Why? Didn't he have to sign for them?"

"No. He turned the job over to me. Because the request was very specific. The lawyer's letter said not to send the data electronically. They was afraid the problem might be in our computer system and the data could get corrupted again. So, they asked for the original paper reports. Promised to return them when they was finished. That's what O'Malley had me send. The paper reports."

I could see the retelling was pretty emotional for Shirley Mae. She was upset about being fired from a job she loved. In her mind, she had done nothing wrong. She had simply followed orders from her boss.

"Hold up, Shirley Mae. Let's take a break. You getting all this?" I asked Paige.

She nodded. "It's remarkable. So, what I'm hearing is Perkins signed off on the first round of records that were sent electronically, but he wasn't even in town when the hard copies were sent. O'Malley was."

"Truth is always stranger than fiction," I said with a chuckle.

Shirley Mae's mouth was parched, her lips dry, her tongue tied. I buzzed my secretary and asked her to bring in a pitcher of ice water and three tumblers, which she did instantly. I knew Mary was listening in on the intercom, so I asked her to join us. I have very few secrets from Mary regarding our business life. Because there were only two chairs, she took a seat on the window ledge. Her eyes fixed on Shirley Mae.

"How ya doing, Shirley Mae? Doing okay?" she asked in a motherly tone, offering a tissue. Shirley Mae dabbed her eyes.

Sipping her water slowly, Paige studied Mary through the tilted glass, sizing her up as only women can.

"Please continue," I said to Shirley Mae. "Did the original documents ever get returned?"

Shirley Mae set her glass down on the edge of my desk and continued.

"Yes. I saw them when the package came back, about two months later."

"Was there anything different about them? Anything that you could tell was missing?"

"I can't rightly say, Mac. The envelope seemed a little lighter. Thinner, maybe. But I didn't reenter them into our system. I had moved on to another job by then, and some new data entry clerk logged everything in."

"And this clerk has been interviewed by AI?" I inquired, to be sure she wasn't overlooked.

"No."

"Why not?"

"She no longer works at TPD. Don't know where she skipped off to. Last I heard she was headed to San Francisco."

Paige seemed puzzled. "Is that it? It that the end of the story?"

"No. I didn't think about this until yesterday, when O'Malley caught me making my notes. Two days I spent pulling the original paper documents, poring over them, and comparing them to the digital records file we rebuilt at his request. The paper and electronic files matched up perfectly. Name for name, report for report."

Paige followed up. "So, what was the problem that you needed to jot down?"

"Estelle Jenkins' record was not in either. There was no original paper file and no electronic copy."

"That makes sense," noted Paige. "They should be the same."

"Yes," said Shirley. But my neighbor was murdered in 2020. That's a fact. I held the original copy of the serious crime report in my hand before I sent it out to the Justice Department..."

"And it never came back!" I finished for her."

18

. . . .

"So, there could be other records that never got returned."
Mary said what everyone else was thinking.

"But why?" asked Paige. "And how?"

"This is not an occasion we can blame on the United
States Postal Service," I said emphatically. "Someone,
somewhere in the chain during the resubmission process,
pulled out those records for a reason."

"Not just someone," observed Paige. "Someone outside
of TPD."

"Sure looks that way."

"Going forward, how do you think we should handle
this, Mac?" asked Mary.

"Why don't you dig through the old newspapers from
2020. See how many events you can find that year that fit
the 'serious crimes' profile. Especially the homicides."

"Got it."

"Shirley Mae? Do you know the officer who is running
the investigation for IA?"

"Yeah, I do. A man named Connors."

"Can he be trusted?"

"Don't see why not. Seems like a stuffed shirt to me."

"Good. Go to him. Give him your statement. Tell him everything. Word for word, just like you just told us here. It's important he understands the 'big switch,' if that's in fact what did occur, did not happen on Perkins' watch."

"Paige, don't you know someone in the Justice Department?"

"Yes. My brother."

"Call him. See if he can track down that April 2021 letter, or at least the name of the person who sent it."

"Whatcha gon' do, Mac?" asked Shirley Mae.

"I'm going to go see O'Malley, face to face, tell him what I know, and try to reason with him. Get him to see things in another light. Maybe there's still a copy of the letter in a dusty filing cabinet somewhere at police headquarters. He might know."

But first I needed to send an urgent text to William Perkins: "Decision time. Pressure building at TPD. Shirley Mae fired. O'Malley out of his depth! Adult needed!"

Reluctantly, Mary agreed to drive Paige back to her hotel to freshen up and change out of the skirt, blouse and jacket she'd been wearing for three days straight. I noticed she was beginning to keep her distance from others in the room, despite regular showers between lovemaking sessions. The sweet fragrance of Bare Essence never left her, to my olfactive pleasure.

I dreaded squaring off with O'Malley on his own turf. Surely, he would see it as a victory, a sign of his superiority. I saw it as the confrontation it was going to be: me telling him he needed to step up and defend his boss, and reinstate Shirley Mae Brown A.S.A.P. He also needed to sit for his own interview with the IA folks and relate his involvement in the resubmission debacle. Lastly, I needed him to cough up that letter, if it still existed, from the Justice Department requesting the re-submission. That was tantamount to a smoking gun. It may have resulted in a totally innocent loss of records on the Bureau of Justice Statistics' part. But my instincts told me otherwise.

"That's a very entertaining fairy tale, Cole," said O'Malley when I had concluded Shirley Mae's account of the events. I really hated seeing him sitting in the chief's chair with that smug look on his thin, pale face. "You and Shirley Mae will go to any lengths to remove the noose from around Perkins' neck, including concocting one hell of a wild tale. Well, I ain't buying it."

"You don't remember any of it, O'Malley? Seems to me you were at the center of it all at the time. The chief wasn't even in town."

"Can't recall a thing."

"Not even the letter?"

"There was no letter. Shirley Mae made that up when she tossed the records – her neighbor's included – at the request of Chief Perkins. End of story."

"That's the way you see it?"

"That's the way it went down, according to your girlfriend's news article. I didn't make it up. Or didn't you read it?"

"Maybe *she* made it up?"

"Now that's a unique defense. You think IA will go for that one?"

"Listen, O'Malley, use your head. Estelle Jenkins was shot and killed in a drive-by. It was in the papers. It's on the record. It's not a fairy tale."

"I'm not arguing that point. Some officer wrote it up, and one of my detectives investigated it, as he normally would. Both did their job. But Perkins tossed the report along with the others to make himself look good."

"You're hoping IA goes along with that story, and not Shirley Mae's."

"C'mon Cole, you're smarter than that. We all know how Shirley Mae feels about Perkins. If I'm asked Shirley Mae's testimony, that's what I will say to IA."

There was no appealing to O'Malley on any level. His ingrained prejudice and bitterness ran too deep. Another approach was needed.

"You know what I think, O'Malley? Maybe *you* tossed those reports to make your boss look bad."

"Get real, Cole. No one's gonna believe that." He rose from his chair. "Are we through, here?" I could tell he was jonesing for a cigarette.

"Just one more thing. Whether IA believes Shirley Mae Brown's story or not, she had an opportunity to throw you under the bus and didn't take it. What does that tell you about loyalty?"

I left the police station in the same frame of mind as I had arrived in. I knew arguing with O'Malley for the good of the force was a hopeless endeavor, but I had to try.

Outside in the parking lot, storm clouds again gathered overhead. Seems I couldn't shake them. At least this time I was prepared. The Jaguar's top was up.

I started the engine. She purred, just like big cats do when well cared for. I wished I had someone looking after me the way I looked after her.

I dialed the office to see how things went with the two women currently occupying opposing sides in my life. I feared a cat fight lay ahead. Such were the strong emotions I seemed to pull out of adult women who wanted to coddle me. Believe me, I wasn't complaining.

Mary asked, "How did it go with O'Malley? Is he going to reinstate Shirley Mae?"

"She stands a better chance at winning the Preakness," I replied. "A pinhead like O'Malley doesn't suddenly sprout wings. What about you? What did you find out?"

"There were at least seven homicides reported in the Trenton papers in 2020. Eight, including Estelle Jenkins, plus one suspicious SIDS death."

"That's nine in total. Not a lot, by averages, but enough to keep Trenton out of the top spot, if reported correctly. Am I right?"

"Yes. Topeka that year maxed out with six."

"Which is interesting, Mary. In a normal year, nine homicides by itself would draw suspicion from police staff. But zero drew no notice."

"Because of aberrations caused by the pandemic. And because nine is so low, it flew under the radar when they disappeared."

"Which suggests Trenton was targeted."

"Exactly."

"What does our investigative journalist say about your findings?"

"I didn't tell her. I wanted to run it by you first. Besides, she seems distracted. Her brother hasn't called her back yet."

"That doesn't seem odd to me, Mary. These fat cat Washington legal guys make their own rules and schedules. Does it seem odd to you?"

"Not half as odd as you being with her."

"Ah, Mary. Not to worry. We're just professional acquaintances."

"Acquaintances with benefits."

"Did she tell you that?"

"No, you did. When you brought her back to the office with you."

"Where is she now?"

"I dropped her off at Jake's."

"Did she ask you to take her there?"

"No. It was my idea. I figured Nick needed to work on his act with her tonight."

"Mary, you scoundrel."

"That's what you pay me for, Mac. To clean up behind you!"

19

• • • • • • • • • • • •

I found Paige Turner where Mary led me to believe I would find her: seated on the same barstool she had occupied the night I first met her, five days ago. The barstool next to the one reserved for yours truly, near the register where Nick Falcone would stand, on slow nights, counting the evening's liquor receipts while bending my ear with incredible tales of his youthful conquests.

"Excuse me, is this seat taken?" I asked Paige politely.

"It is now," she replied with a warm smile.

I slid into my usual seat whereupon I was rewarded with a tender kiss on the cheek from Paige and a double Jack Daniels on the rocks from Nick. As expected, the kiss elicited a comment from Nick.

"Ho, ho, ho, I see this relationship has advanced a step or two since last week. Do tell."

"Mind your own damn business, barkeep," I snapped jokingly.

"Actually, your lady friend has already filled me in on your recent adventures along Great Bay and LBI. Did anyone ask for me while you were staying at the Surf City Hotel?"

I wondered just how "adventurous" Paige made our time together sound to Nick the gossip. I'm glad he didn't say exploits. Then I would have known for sure I was in trouble.

"Yeah, Detective O'Malley asked about you. You're wanted for questioning regarding the alarming number of naked female bodies that have been washing ashore."

"Mermaids all," Paige teased.

"My kind of catch," countered Nick before he sauntered off to fetch another Jägermeister for a gray-bearded customer. I motioned to Nick to put it on my tab. The old man tipped his shot glass my way. "Down the hatch she goes, mate," he said before giving it a proper sendoff.

"Do you always do that?" Paige asked, noting what had become a nightly ritual. "It's charming."

"No. Only when a pretty lady is sitting next to me."

Paige smiled. She looked refreshed. Showered. A new white blouse with a black blazer and tight blue jeans. I sat back and wafted the Bare Essence, letting the memories come flooding back to me.

"Mary tells me you've been having trouble getting hold of your brother."

"What else did Mary tell you?"

"That there were at least eight or nine homicides in Trenton in 2020, and if I'm not careful, I could be a statistic this year."

"That sounds like Mary."

"She really is a sweetheart and extremely efficient."

"Yes. Your Miss Moneypenny."

"Is it my car, or my boudoir fare that reminds you of James Bond?"

"It's the total picture, James."

"Just what I wanted to grow up to be. Every woman's fantasy."

"Keep deluding yourself, Mac."

My turn to throw something down the hatch. "A toast to the grand delusion of life!"

Paige continued. "So, anyway, Mary's report notwithstanding, Penrose finally got back to me. He said he would check into the letter but not to get our hopes up. He claimed that, from the sound of its contents, a letter of that nature from over two years ago has probably been tossed as a matter of course."

"I thought governmental agencies were required to retain records for seven years."

"I did, too. But when I asked him about that, he said the letter is what they commonly refer to as a "one-off," meaning it's not likely to be repeated because it's not very important. Like a memo."

"Hmm. But what if TPD didn't comply? Would there have been a follow-up?"

"He didn't say, and I didn't get into it with him. I got the impression he was pressed for time. Any luck with O'Malley?"

"Yeah, he now qualifies as a super flaming asshole. He wouldn't budge. Totally unmoved by Shirley Mae's story. He labeled it a 'fairy tale.' He seemed to have an answer for everything, with the O'Malley take on life built right into it. He's made up his mind that this mess is all Perkins' handiwork and Perkins got caught."

"Did I hear you mention Chief Perkins?" asked Nick, sliding down the bar with fresh drinks in hand. "He came in here earlier today looking for you, Mac. On the QT. Didn't want anyone to see him. Only stayed a minute or two."

"When?"

"Just before the lady arrived. It was a good thing the two of you didn't run into each other. Sparks would have flown for sure."

"I was down at headquarters trying to put a round peg in a square hole named O'Malley. What did Perkins want? Did he say anything?"

"Only that this town was in more disarray than Poughkeepsie ever was."

"What?" Paige and I shouted in unison.

"What did him mean by Poughkeepsie?" I demanded.

"The town in New York."

"I know where it is. What did he mean by it?"

"You mean you don't know? He never told you? Here, I thought you two were drinking buddies, thick as thieves. You need to come over to my side of the bar occasionally, Mac. You just might learn something."

"Tell us about Poughkeepsie, Nick. What did you learn from Perkins?"

"That's where he was stationed as a rookie cop. Before he came to Trenton. While he was there he got a commendation for exemplary service, which he was able to parlay, after several years of distinguished service here, into the chief's position when it opened up."

...

We didn't stay to finish our drinks.

"It's got to be a coincidence," Paige said as we pulled out of the parking lot. Destination unknown. We just needed a quiet place to talk it out, away from the town gossip. No offense to Nick. He holds a plethora of vital information in that warped mind of his. I just didn't want our conversation to become the latest addition.

"Which part?" I said in answer to Paige's question. Poughkeepsie, the Black rookie cop, or the commendation part?"

"All of it. It still doesn't tie in. One event involved three teens and an alleged vagrant homicide. The other is about underreporting crime data."

"Homicide data, Paige."

"But what's the 'connective tissue' that ties the two together?"

"I'm guessing it's Perkins."

"To a novel written by my father over thirty years ago?"

"To the actual set of events the book's based on. You must admit it's awfully odd that both the book and the idea for your exposé came up at the same time between your father and brother before it occurred to Peters."

"But the *U.S. News'* statistics appeared months earlier. You could say years earlier, when the data was collected. That had nothing to do with the three of them."

"Planning played a part."

"By whom? The *U.S. News* reporter? The National Crime Bureau?"

"The Justice Department," I said emphatically.

"Oh please, Mac! Listen to yourself. You sound like one of those MAGA conspiracy nuts."

"I need to see that letter. You need to talk to your father."

"That's not as easy as it sounds. He's getting up in years. We're growing distant. I thought my doing the Trenton piece would bring us closer, since he basically suggested it."

"Has it?"

"We're as distant as ever. I communicate with him through Penrose. He's my dad's 'pride and joy.'"

"What kind of relationship do you have with your brother?"

"No better. Mary was right. I was totally bummed when I couldn't reach Penrose right away. I couldn't help thinking he was giving me the bum's rush while we were on the phone. I could almost see him anxiously pacing as we spoke."

"You need to reach out to your dad. And I need to sit down with Perkins."

"Now?"

"The sooner the better. The hearing could be any day now with Perkins back in town."

"What about dinner?"

"It's either a rain check or fast-food drive-through."

"I'll take the rain check."

"I'll drop you off at your hotel. Where are you staying?"

"The Marriot in Ewing. Near the airport."

"You're kidding."

"No, why?"

"I'm staying there."

"Why are you staying there?"

"I live there. Ever since my home was torched by a couple of thugs a few years back during another missing person's case I was involved in. Suite 3C is home, sweet home."

"You're pulling my leg."

I sure would like to, and then some. Alas, business before pleasure. "No, really."

"I'm in 6C. Three doors down."

"Another coincidence? Imagine that."

"How about, after you see Perkins and I make my call, we meet up in my suite for a nightcap."

"Sounds 'suite' to me. I'll bring the prosecco."

"I'll have on Bare Essence, so you can just follow your nose."

"I'll do exactly that."

20

••••••••••

I texted Perkins in case he was indisposed, say, meeting with his lawyer. He said he wasn't home. His place was too hot. The circus had arrived. A horde of paparazzi and newshounds were camped on his front yard waiting for his eventual return.

He asked if we could meet at my place. With Paige Turner, his favorite investigative reporter just three doors away, I didn't think that was a good idea. I didn't tell him that, of course. I told him the maid service had been neglectful lately and the place was a pigsty.

I suggested we meet at a neutral location, such as Mary Porter's house, in twenty minutes and gave him the address. He agreed. I then phoned Mary to clear it with her. She asked if Paige would be coming with me. I told her Paige was ensconced in her room at the hotel for the evening. Mary said in that case the front door would be open.

I asked her to order a couple pizzas and charge them to the firm. Then I stopped to pick up a six-pack. Michelobs. I remembered from our recent meeting on Bill's boat that was his beer of choice.

Bill arrived first. He waited until he saw the Jag pull up before he got out of his truck. He gave me a broad smile when he saw the six-pack tucked under my arm. We embraced.

Mary greeted us at the door and led us into the kitchen. The pizzas were stacked and steaming on the table. Mary set out paper plates and napkins. We each declined glasses for our beers.

"They won't have time to sit around and get warm," Perkins joked. In the glare of the bright kitchen light, he looked thinner and, if possible for a Black man, paler than last time I saw him, only yesterday. Obviously, the investigation was taking its toll on the dedicated police chief.

As Mary was leaving the kitchen, Bill grabbed her arm to stop her. "I've got nothing to say that you can't hear, Mary," he said tenderly. She took a seat next to me and grabbed a beer.

"I have a confession to make," Bill started. "I lied to you, Mac. Back there on the boat. I told you I didn't know about the book, *Dark Mercy*. That was a lie."

The admission prompted questions. But I kept quiet. This was Perkins' show. He needed to have his say.

"In fact, as you may know, the book, packaged as fiction, is about me. More to the point, it's about an incident I was involved in as a rookie cop in 1993 back in Poughkeepsie, New York."

He took a long pull on his beer. Mary was too enrapt to eat. But story time never diminished my appetite. I ate. We both waited for him to continue.

"Three Black teens were accused of brutally attacking and killing a homeless vagrant, a strung-out military veteran named Johnny Wise. The kids were accused of killing him with a kitchen knife during a scuffle that ensued when they tried to relieve him of his drugs. That ain't what happened."

He paused and bit into a slice of pie, chewing it slowly, then another bite, and swallowed before he continued. The hot pizza with friends must have been his first decent meal in a week. He seemed to savor it.

"You have to understand, Poughkeepsie back in the nineties was not what you would call a progressive town. Not socially. Not racially. Law enforcement and the judicial system were stacked against Blacks, Hispanics and just about every other non-white race. At first, I thought it would be a challenge for me. That's why I applied there after the academy. I couldn't have anticipated the nightmare it truly was. Corruption ran rampant, with the full knowledge and support of the very people sworn to protect and serve *all* people within their jurisdiction.

The defendants didn't stand a chance in the system. A white American ex-soldier, a decorated veteran, no less, was dead in an alley in a Black neighborhood."

Perkins finished his slice and opened another beer.

"Following a 911 call, my partner of just one day and I were the first to arrive at the scene. I covered the rear of the alley while my partner charged in head-on. A corpse, a bloody knife, and three stultified, shell-shocked teens stood over the body.

"In his report, my partner said he saw one of the teens drop the knife. It was the same teen who was found to have coke on him. My partner said all three kids were 'high as kites.' I questioned the kids myself. They were scared but lucid. They told me the white cop kicked the knife in the direction of the kid whose fingerprints were said to be found on the knife. He told me he may have picked it up just to move it away. He couldn't recall clearly.

"Separately, each one told me the same story. That they were walking home through the alley. That this crazed vagrant came running up to them and demanded drugs. When they refused, the bum pulled out a knife and, in the tussle that followed, he got stabbed. They admitted the coke was theirs, but insisted the murder was purely an accident. That it occurred while they tried to defend themselves.

"At the trial it would come down to the word of three young Black drug users roaming the alleyways at night against the word of the white ex-Marine cop. Whose word is the jury gonna believe?"

Perkins set his beer bottle down.

"I know which story I believed. At the time, evidence room procedures were pretty lax. An officer could sign in and review the evidence collected at a crime in order to make sure his report was accurate. One day I was granted access to the room. I don't know if there were prints on the knife or not. Or whose they were, or how they got there. When I left the room, no one's fingerprints were on that knife.

At the pre-trial hearing, the prosecution realized they had nothing but a simple drug possession case. To placate a growing uprising in the Black community the prosecution dropped all charges."

"You tampered with evidence, Bill," I said. "That's a crime."

"I showed them mercy, Mac. In a judicial system that is supposed to be colorblind. Dark mercy!"

"Like the book title," noted Mary. "Did you suggest it to the author?"

"No. But my partner may have. I'm sure he surmised what was done but could never prove it. He also knew I had the goods on him. So, he kept quiet, except for spilling his guts to the author, who treated the story as fiction."

"Like the evidence planting?" I proffered.

Perkins finished his beer. "I take it you read the book."

"No. Paige did. She gave me the CliffsNotes version when we went looking for you. What I want to know is how the author Martin L. Turner got involved to begin with."

Mary looked perplexed. "Turner. Is he related to Paige?"

"He's her father."

"Oh boy." Mary took a swig of her beer. "Now *this* is getting interesting."

"Did you know that, Bill, when you saw her exposé?"

"I assumed so, after recognizing the last name when she was attempting to contact me. Shirley Mae used the internet to confirm it for me."

I shook my head. "But it still gets back to the question of why did Martin Turner get involved in the story in the first place? Of all the crimes occurring in America daily during that time, why choose that one? Surely, there were other, more intriguing cases to write about. What led him to write about the Poughkeepsie incident?"

"I don't know for certain, Mac. But I hear tell he paid for the vagrant's funeral service and made sure he was buried in the military cemetery."

"Why? Was it in conjunction with some charitable cause he believed in?"

"My sources tell me he and Johnny Wise served together in Kuwait. They were in the same unit. Turner got out and went on to become a writer. Wise stayed in and got lost. But apparently, they never lost touch."

"That's very interesting. Now I see the connection."

"Do you think Paige knows?" asked Mary.

Good question, Mary. "I don't think so. If she did, I don't think she would have hung around here."

Mary chuckled. "Maybe she had other reasons."

"She's not a poker player, Mary."

"And neither are you, Mac."

"Enough, you two," said Perkins, snapping us back to the conversation at hand. "If this data sifting scam was done for revenge purposes, we can safely assume Martin Turner is the architect. But who helped him pull it off?"

Mary asked, "You don't believe it was an inside job, through O'Malley?"

Perkins laughed. "O'Malley is many things I don't particularly care for, but he is not a schemer. Sure, he says he wants my job. Give him two days and he'll want to give it back."

"We just concluded that Martin Turner was the architect, the planner, but we need grunts to do the heavy lifting."

"Right. But O'Malley is no one's lackey, either."

"He could have been tricked into being complicit," offered Mary.

I jumped in. "Not according to Shirley Mae. She claims he delegated the records resubmission project then as he has this investigation. To others."

The light suddenly went on. I looked at Perkins. "That's why you left him in charge. In full view of everyone. But you said you smelled a rat."

"Yes, but I didn't necessarily mean in the TPD."

"Then where?" Mary asked.

Perkins rolled it over in his mind. "Where indeed?"

I stood up, nearly falling backwards with the "Eureka!" moment. "The Justice Department."

"Of course," acknowledged Mary. "And now we know who fits in those Cinderella slippers."

"Penrose Turner. Paige's brother," I said to a confused but suddenly relieved Chief Bill Perkins.

"Can we prove it?" he asked.

"I'm betting we can, if we can get our hands on a certain letter, Bill. The one from the Justice Department that arrived when you were on vacation back in April of 2021. The letter requesting the resubmission of records to the Bureau of Justice Statistics, an agency that falls under jurisdiction of the Justice Department, who subsequently returned the original TPD paper documents, minus a few choice homicide reports, guaranteeing to put you in the hot seat you're in today."

"I guess there's no chance in hell Paige's brother is going to find that letter for us." Mary was spot on.

"Chief," I said, "we need O'Malley. Your future, the future of the TPD and the entire city, rests on the shoulders of Detective Gregory O'Malley and whatever he does in the next twenty-four hours."

"Why in the next twenty-four hours?" asked Mary.

"Tell her, Chief."

"The hearing with Internal Affairs has been scheduled for Thursday morning."

21

. . . .

All the pieces were beginning to fall neatly into place. We now had a fairly accurate picture of what had transpired in the data scam and why. What we didn't have was concrete evidence to pin it on the real perpetrators. The smoking gun. That piece, if it even still existed, rested in the hands of the one person I had acknowledged from the start had the most to gain from ousting Bill Perkins as Police Chief, and therefore was the least likely to cooperate on the side of the defense in any way, shape, or form.

At this point we knew the reason for the switcheroo: revenge. More precisely, to rectify a perceived injustice. We knew the mastermind. Martin L. Turner. He wrote about it because it stuck in his craw. But the book drew little attention to Johnny Wise's ugly fate, perhaps because it was shielded by the long arm of the law and couched in fictional terms.

What we had yet to prove was how the Justice Department became a cog in this wheel of illicit events. Odds favored Penrose Turner somehow. But who else?

These were the thoughts running through my mind as I sped away from our pizza party at Mary Porter's. We had the bases covered, but the cleanup hitter had yet to decide whether to step up to the plate.

I was quite certain much of this would come as a surprise to Paige, and not a very pleasant one. I was therefore reluctant to discuss any of it with her tonight. I didn't know if she got in touch with her father and had that frank father-to-daughter talk about the turn of events. I was doubtful it took place.

I glanced at my watch. Ten p.m. Paige would be up. I had bought the prosecco when I bought the Michelob, so I was reasonably prepared for our planned romantic rendezvous – only, my heart wasn't in it. More to the point, neither was my mind or any other part of my anatomy at this juncture. I was thousands of miles away on the shore of uncertainty. Uncertain about the future. Mine and several others'.

The fate of Chief Bill Perkins was certainly foremost on my mind. So was that of Shirley Mae Brown. Two would-be victims as a consequence of two men's decisions to take the law into their own hands, Bill Perkins and Martin L. Turner.

The unintended consequences and the victims in that fallout were less obvious. Gary Peters, for one, possibly. Paige Turner, for sure. I couldn't help feeling she'd been duped. Worse, by her own family. She didn't deserve that. True, she was caught up in it, and complicit, to a point. But she had tried to exercise some professional due diligence, albeit in the eleventh hour. She knew something wasn't quite kosher. Something was rotten in Denmark – or Trenton, as the case may be.

This brought me back to my near-future personal plans. I've never been one to pass up a roll in the hay when it's offered. Unlike Nick Falcone, my sexual interludes were few and far between. But what Nick and I did share was an aversion to commitment. For different reasons.

Nick liked to play the field. To be fair, maybe he simply hadn't found the right field. Me, I'm just not a team player. Not anymore. I've been through a marriage. That hurt. Been part of a large corporation. That hurt more. I suppose I grew out of both painfully, same way a boy outgrows childhood and becomes a man. It was time to concentrate on my own needs. Life was simpler that way.

Maybe O'Malley had reached the same point in life. Although he'd certainly taken a different route to reach it and seemed to have a different attitude about it. Maybe he had tried the "rah-rah-go-team" thing and became frustrated when he saw so many around him not pulling their own weight. Pulling him down. Hard to say. Despite O'Malley's many flaws, Perkins still saw good in him. Like Darth Vader. A hard and bitter exterior, protecting a molten core of goodness, given over to the dark side.

I knew Paige would be disappointed, or pissed, or both. Screw it. I would deal with her in the morning, along with the other important matters pending. Right now, I didn't need a woman. I needed the type of comfort only Tennessee whiskey could bring. A half-mile from the Marriott, I improvised a K-turn in the middle of Scotch Road and redirected the Jaguar onto a fond and familiar route toward Jake's.

The place was jumping but sparsely populated. It was, after all, a Tuesday night. Holly and the Headliners were just finishing up their final set. She had everybody rocking with her version of "Crazy." A few patrons hustled to the bar for one more round before their imminent departures.

My "reserved" barstool was vacant. But I noticed the one to its right, Paige's seat lately, was occupied. The torso looked familiar, but it sure as hell was not that of Paige Turner.

"What are you doing here, O'Malley?" I said with obvious annoyance.

"What's it look like I'm doing? I'm having a drink."

"Why here?"

"I've got the hots for Holly."

"Who doesn't?"

I caught Nick's eye and raised two fingers. I needed a double on the double.

I slid onto my seat. "Tough day at the office?"

"Nothing I can't handle."

"You know Perkins is back in town."

"I've heard."

"The hearing's set for Thursday."

"Heard that too."

Nick nodded and set the drink down in front of me. "Second time tonight, Mac. We're honored. Maybe you'll finish your drink this time and not waste good whiskey," he added before slipping off.

I gave Nick a wink and took a slow sip. It burned going down, letting me know my troubles would soon be gone. Except maybe for the one sitting next to me.

"Where's your girlfriend?" O'Malley asked. He was nursing a Michelob. Just another coincidence in a day in a life chock full of coincidences.

"Getting her beauty sleep, I'd imagine."

"Seems to be working so far." That made me chuckle.

"You saw Perkins tonight."

From his delivery, I couldn't tell if he was asking me or stating a fact.

"He likes Mics, too." That got a chuckle out of O'Malley.

"What do you think his chances are?"

I wasn't sure the nature of O'Malley's question, so I asked, "... of surviving the investigation, you mean?"

"What else would I be asking?"

Nothing, asshole, but why ask me? "What I think doesn't matter, does it?"

"Well maybe in this case I'd like to hear it."

"Truthfully, he could use a hand. I think you know what I mean."

O'Malley grew wistful. "Perkins and I have been on the force together for over twenty years. Practically started out together as beat cops pounding the sidewalks, handling crowd control during parades, directing traffic. Then we went our separate ways. Me to vice and him into the squad car. When we both made sergeant, he took a desk job and I went the detective route. I needed to be outdoors."

"To pollute your lungs," I said, referring to his tobacco addiction. "You know it's going to catch up with you at some point."

"Yeah, well, we all have to go sometime."

He took a sip of his beer. I noticed it was still three quarters full and wondered how many he had had before I arrived.

"Anyway," he continued, "when Perkins made chief, I was upset. You know that. Everyone knew that. I thought I deserved it. You didn't know me back then, Cole, but I was a good cop. I took it hard."

O'Malley began picking at the label on the bottle, searching for the right words to continue. "In time I came to realize the mayor and city council had made the right choice. The city was changing. I wasn't the right person for the job. Perkins kept the lid on things, especially the political stuff. Man, that shit sucks. But he handles it."

I took a slow sip of my drink and waited for him to continue.

"I guess you're wondering where I'm going with all this?"

No, butthead, the thought hadn't crossed my mind. I spent a good part of this afternoon trying to appeal to your better angels, to no avail. Why now?

He pushed the bottle away and put a curled fifty down on the bar. "I guess what I'm trying to say, Cole, is this isn't the way it should end for a good cop like Perkins. He doesn't deserve it. Trenton doesn't deserve it. He's dedicated his life to the citizens of this town because, unlike me, he thinks they're worth it. I wish I had his conviction."

O'Malley reached into his jacket pocket, pulled out an envelope and handed it to me.

"I'm leaving this in your hands, for you to give to Shirley Mae Brown when she returns to her post tomorrow. Tell her to make sure she brings it to the hearing on Thursday. I hope it helps."

He slid off his stool, clasped me on the shoulder, and left.

I opened the white envelope. Inside was a one-page typed letter on Bureau of Justice Statistics letterhead, bearing the U.S. Department of Justice seal. It was dated April 21, 2021, tersely advising the Trenton Police Department of the receipt of their unreadable data by the National Crime Bureau, requesting the resubmission of the authentic paper reports. The material would be treated with due confidentiality and returned forthwith. Nearly verbatim as Shirley Mae had recounted to us. The letter was signed by the Attorney for Departmental Records, Penrose M. Turner, Esq.

I was pondering O'Malley's sudden and unexpected change of heart when Nick came to collect the fifty-dollar bill.

"How many beers did he have?" I asked Nick.

He pointed to the mostly-full bottle. "Just one. And that's it.

22

. . . .

I stayed up half the night wondering how I was going to tell Paige Turner all I had learned while she was playing tiddlywinks in her hotel room. Bailing on our date was the easy part. It was business. The fact that I didn't call to let her know might be a bit dicey.

But how do you tell a woman you've known less than a week, a woman you have been intimate with and may have some feelings for, that her father and brother have been implicated in a criminal act? It was hard to say until it all shook out and the dust settled. Conceivably, she might be an unwitting co-conspirator. Yikes!

The direct route would be to show her the letter. With it, her brother had signed his own death warrant. But what if she went ballistic and ripped it up? Or took it and ran to her father and brother to get back in their good graces.

I needn't have worried. She was as smart as any woman I'd ever met. My standing her up last night was an awakening. She woke up in the morning prepared for bad news and ready to exercise her independence.

I went to her room but she wasn't there. I checked the buffet area. Not there, either. Finally, I went to the first place I should have looked. The Fitness Center. She was dressed in tight black spandex, using the elliptical. She caught my reflection in the mirror as I walked in behind her. We were alone.

She stopped when she saw me. My mannerisms must have been a dead giveaway, because she quickly halted my advance. I didn't expect a kiss or a hug, but the hand was totally unexpected.

"Stop right there. Before you say anything, hear me out."

I sat down on one of the power benches.

"I don't care that you stood me up last night. I don't care that you didn't call. I don't even care that you showed up here this morning without a bouquet of flowers. What I'm upset about is that you didn't trust me enough to include me in your clandestine activities. You forget, McKenzie Cole, that I have a stake in whatever is going on, and that means in whatever you found out. Whatever people told you firsthand, I had a right to know. No! I had a right to hear it from them directly. It was my exposé that started all this. Or don't you remember?"

I stood there like a stone, agape, knowing she was absolutely right. She was entitled to all of it. But none of it would have come out if she had been present. Especially from Bill Perkins, and especially now that we know what we know. How could he trust anyone with the surname Turner?

"So, I've made my decision. I'm not going to wait around for the hearing. Whatever happens, happens. I called this morning. I'm booked on the seven p.m. flight to Kansas City. What do you say to that?"

What could I say? "I'll drive you to the airport. I wish you would reconsider. The hearing is scheduled for tomorrow."

"Too late, Mac. My mind is made up."

"Did you talk to your father last night? Did he ask you to come home?" It was a shot in the dark, but something in her demeanor suggested this was not a unilateral decision.

"He's not doing well. And yes, he asked me, not Penrose this time, to come look after him."

"I see. Of course. If he's not well, you've got to go to him. Did you ask him about Poughkeepsie and the catalyst for his writing a thinly veiled book about it?"

"He said he read about it in the newspaper. It seemed interesting to him at the time."

"Did he ever mention the name Johnny Wise to you?"

"Johnny and Dad were in Desert Storm together. In Dad's study there's a picture of the two of them together and another of their whole unit."

"Anything else? Did you ever meet him? Did your dad ever say what might have happened to him?"

"Dad left the Marine Corps. Johnny stayed. That's all I know. Why all the questions about Johnny Wise?"

"You read the book *Dark Mercy*. Do you remember the name of the homeless vet the teens were accused of killing?"

"Ah yeah, Jimmie DeWitt, I think. Why?"

"Seems pretty close to the name Johnny Wise, doesn't it?"

"I guess. Dad probably had his old Marine buddy in mind when he fictionalized the story."

"No doubt."

"Is there a point to this game of twenty questions, Mac? I'd like to get another mile or two in on the elliptical before breakfast."

"There's a little coffee shop around the corner called Kristie's Café. They have an assortment of fruit-filled pastries and a rack of herbal teas."

"You buying?"

"It's the least I can do after you've put up with me for nearly a week."

"Yeah, I'm going to miss you, too, Mac. I'll meet you in the lobby in about twenty minutes."

...

The reconciliation went more smoothly than I expected. Paige bared her claws and got her shots in, but I came through it alright. I was disappointed to hear she was going back to Kansas but not surprised that Daddy played the sick card to hurry her along. I had planted the seed of the Johnny Wise/ Jimmie DeWitt connection. I would lay some more groundwork at breakfast. Enough to get her to reconsider her flight back to Kansas if necessary.

I went back to my room and took a cold shower. Women in spandex have that effect on me, especially when observed exercising from behind. I shaved and gave my mustache a quick trim, then headed out to the lobby.

I knew I was in trouble when, thirty minutes later, Paige hadn't showed. I went to her room and knocked. No answer. I went back down to the lobby and asked the Pakistani concierge if he'd seen the lady in 6C this morning. "Gone," he said. "She left in a cab forty-five minutes ago."

"Did she happen to say where she was going?"

"Not to me," he replied, "but I'm sure the cabby knows." Smartass dothead.

I was getting the distinct impression that Paige had deliberately given me the slip. I asked the concierge if he remembered which cab company had picked her up.

"Diamond," he said.

I asked the dispatcher at Diamond Cab for the destination of the taxi that had just picked up the fare at the Marriot. After a brief silence he said, "That was #161. Omar," he said. "He's enroute to the Trenton-Mercer Airport."

I thanked him and hung up. Then I dialed Frontier Airlines. I was certain Paige said she had booked an evening flight. Was that a lie, too?

My old buddy Cliffy answered the phone. I never gave him my name and he didn't seem to recognize my voice. He confirmed the seven p.m. departure for Kansas City. Did I want to book it? No.

"What's going out in the next hour?" I asked.

A flight was leaving for Tampa at nine-forty-five a.m. They also had an inbound flight from Washington D.C. due to arrive around ten-fifteen a.m. Then nothing until the afternoon. The D.C. flight had to be her target. It could only mean one thing. Paige had reached out to her brother Penrose, and whatever was discussed was important enough to get him to fly up to Trenton, pronto. She said in their conversation yesterday he had seemed dismissive. What changed? Was that conversation a cover? Instinctively, I felt for the envelope in my breast pocket. It was still there.

Mary called to tell me she had heard from Shirley Mae, who had been given her old job back. O'Malley had directed her to come to the station in the afternoon but first to stop and pick something up at my office.

"Do you know anything about that, Mac?" Mary asked.

"Indeed, I do, Mary. Now I believe in miracles, same as you."

"Did I miss something last night? Like a falling star?"

"O'Malley came through. We've got the letter. That's what Shirley Mae needs to pick up. For tomorrow's hearing. It's central to her testimony."

"Oh, happy days, Mac. Does it implicate someone from the Justice Department? Do we have a name to go with the letter?"

"Turner. Penrose Turner. And I believe he's on his way to Trenton to stonewall the proceedings, or clear his name."

"How did he find out, Mac?"

"It pains me to say this, but I suspect Paige has not been straight with us. Perhaps from the start."

"That doesn't surprise me, Mac. I felt something was off about her."

"Your instincts serve you well, Obi Wan. I think we're about to find out just how well, today or tomorrow at the hearing."

"What are you going to do next, Mac?"

"I'm going to see if I can get hold of Bill Perkins. Wish I knew where he was staying."

"He's at my place. Came back after you left. Said he couldn't go home. He couldn't have gotten past the paparazzi, even if he wanted to."

"Mary, you're an angel of mercy."

"Yeah, right. After last night, that word has a whole new meaning. You better be careful how you use it."

...

I caught up with Chief Perkins in the cab of his pickup truck as he was leaving Mary's house.

"Sleep well?" I asked.

"Like a baby," he replied. "First time in a week."

"Where you headed now?"

"City hall. Mayor asked me to come by and bring him up to speed on the latest developments. Gil Hasbrouck has always been in my corner. City council may be a tougher nut to crack."

"You could use all the friends you can get right about now."

"Did you give the letter to my little butterball?"

"Shirley Mae is supposed to stop by the office on her way back to her job at the station. I still can't believe O'Malley had a change of heart."

"Funny what a man will do when the doctors find a spot on your lung."

"Cancer?"

"Stage two."

"You knew?"

"It was obvious. Man was acting more irritable than usual."

"So, his behavior in your absence was all an act."

"We needed to smoke rats out of their holes. No telling who it might be down at headquarters. O'Malley played his part to the hilt."

"Gotta hand it to you, Bill. You handled that pretty darn well."

"Not really. That's why I had to get away for a while. And it's not over yet. Let's see how it goes at the hearing tomorrow."

"That's why I'm here. I came to warn you. The Justice Department official who sent that letter is Penrose Turner. Paige's brother."

"Guess you could say it's a family affair."

"That's not all. He's headed for Trenton as we speak."

"Let him come. This is my town. He's about to find out how we do things in Trenton when we're crossed. And the sister?"

"Wish I could say she's with us. But she may have re-crossed sides.

"Blood is thicker than water."

"Bad blood may be the thickest of all."

Perkins was about to pull away when his cell phone rang. I waited for him to take the call.

He rolled down his window.

"That was the mayor. Looks like your warning comes a beat behind. Turner has asked the mayor and council for a private meeting in advance of the hearing regarding my competency as chief. Says he has incriminating evidence relating to my past service."

"That has to be about Poughkeepsie and *Dark Mercy.*"

"No doubt. Gil was overruled by the council and the meeting was granted. It's set for three p.m. this afternoon. My presence has been requested to hear the accusations."

"Bill, I'd like to tag along for moral support."

"Be my guest, if they'll let you in. The more the merrier. Oh, and one more thing. Gil says the public has gotten wind of the meeting. Two camps of protesters are forming on the front steps. Those who want me to continue as chief and those who want to lynch me. It could get ugly. I'm to use the rear entrance."

"I'll be right behind you."

23

· · · · · · · · · · · ·

I stopped by the office and gave Mary the letter to give to Shirley Mae, then turned and headed back out the door. I didn't even check messages.

"Where to this time?" asked Mary. I could tell she was a little piqued.

"There's fireworks brewing at city hall."

"What should I tell your two o'clock? Mr. Snyder. He was one of the ones we rescheduled from Monday while you were off gallivanting."

Leroy Snyder was a local car dealer. He did pretty well for himself. Married three times, each new wife got progressively younger, and progressively richer despite well-intended prenups. He suspected wife number three was having an affair with one of his young salesmen and asked me to get the goods for him to use in the divorce. Which I reluctantly did, for a ridiculous fee. A PI's gotta eat.

Unfortunately, Mrs. Snyder's lover turned out not to be the young buck salesman, but Leroy Jr. I'd been putting off telling Leroy Sr., hoping he would find out on his own. Their trysts took place not in some seedy hotel but at the Snyder home, after the old man left for work each morning.

Mary disapproved of the delay. Half the town already knew. It was old news. She felt Leroy Sr. might renege on paying my fee if a neighbor decided to tattle.

"Let's reschedule him for the same time tomorrow afternoon. The Perkins' hearing will be over by then. I'll be freed up to pursue regular work and meet with clients again. Tell him to bring his son along."

By the time I got downtown, the shit had hit the fan. Protestors, shouting obscenities and holding up signs on both sides of the steps of city hall were cordoned off with police barricades. The police, in riot gear, held up bulletproof shields and night sticks. One group wanted Chief Perkins hung on the spot. "String him up," was their slogan. Many held up effigies on broomsticks of a black dummy with a noose around his neck and signs declaring, "Time for a clean sweep at the TPD."

The other group comprised mostly Black citizens in support of Chief Perkins. They wanted "Justice for the Just," "Pride, Not Prejudice" and "Innocent Until Proven Guilty."

I parked the Jaguar well out of harm's way and walked the seven blocks back to city hall. The front doors were blocked by Trenton's finest. I tried the rear doors. Also guarded.

A woman and a man encircled by the officers stood near the rear doors, demanding entry. The woman I recognized immediately as Paige Turner in a peacock blue sweater and black skirt with heels to match. The man beside her in the three-piece suit, briefcase in hand, was obviously her twin brother, Penrose. He had the same piercing blue eyes and sandy brown hair. Only his was a combover fanning in the wind.

While one of the officers checked their credentials, another got on the radio to confirm their clearance. I slipped in between them and confronted Paige. "Aren't you going to introduce me?" I quipped.

Penrose looked down his nose at me as Paige made the introductions. He was obviously not impressed. Neither was I.

The guard waved Paige and Penrose forward. Paige grabbed my arm and pulled me along. "He's with us," she said as we passed through the door.

"What's going on?" a befuddled Penrose Turner asked Paige as a quartet of uniformed cops whisked us down the hallway.

"You don't need to know," she replied under her breath.

Penrose wasn't the only one confused. "What *is* going on?" I repeated Penrose's question.

"You should know," came her curt reply.

We were checked again for ID when we got to the open doors of the council room. Inside I could see Mayor Gil Hasbrouck, Chief Perkins, and the five city council members: two men and three women, one from each of the four wards, plus one at-large. Also present were several members of the IA unit, including a graying man with a buzz cut and an erect military bearing I presumed was IA Chief Jack Connors.

Paige and Penrose were let through. I was halted. Paige looked back and shrugged.

"Your name's not on the list," a young officer advised me.

"Surely, that's a mistake. I'm Cole. McKenzie Cole. Chief Perkins' attorney." I said it loudly enough to be heard in the conference room. A bit brazen, perhaps. But I'd gotten this far. No time for civility now.

Perkins looked up, saw me, and whispered something to the mayor. Hasbrouck nodded and waved to the patrolman to let me pass.

The twelve of us took our seats around a large oval table in the center of the room. The mayor at one end with a stenographer behind him. Connors at the other end after his staff departed. The three council women alongside Paige and her brother on one side, and the two men beside Perkins. I was given a folding chair and told to sit behind Perkins. Four officers guarded the doorway: two on each side of the threshold.

Hasbrouck banged the gavel three times and said, "This meeting will now come to order." The doors to the conference room were closed.

"Members of council, distinguished guests." I looked around the table: The Martins and Connors. Did that not include me?

"On the eve of the Internal Affairs investigation hearing scheduled for tomorrow to determine what, if any, role Chief William Perkins played in underreporting 'serious crimes' to the National Crime Bureau in 2020, I have been asked by the United States Justice Department, represented today by Penrose M. Turner Esquire, to convene this special meeting of the Trenton City Council to hear testimony from both Mr. Turner and his sister, Ms. Paige Turner, concerning Chief William Perkins' alleged past criminal behavior as an officer of the law. Mr. Turner, the floor is yours."

Wow! A bold accusation on the eve of the police's own internal hearing. Worse, in my mind, that Paige had crossed a line and was part of it. However, looking around the room gave me encouragement. The Turners had seriously misgauged the sociopolitical makeup of the

Trenton community and the city administration's current ethnic balance.

Chief Perkins and four of the five council members were Black, and one was an Italian restaurant owner named Tucci from the south ward. In addition to the restaurateur were the openly gay white mayor, IA Chief Connors, and the two Turners – both out-of-towners. Had Penrose failed to do his homework? Where, I wondered, did that leave the consensus in the room, if you included me and the white female stenographer? I noticed Turner perspiring just a little in his tailored clothes as he began to speak.

"As many of you know, Lady Justice with her balanced scales is depicted blindfolded, to remind us that justice is blind to all manner of human prejudice while upholding the rule of law. Chaos would reign otherwise. It is imperative that members of law enforcement and the judicial system are likewise blind when meting out consequences. Life is untenable when officials lead wild-west-style. I'm here to tell you Chief William Perkins did just that, thirty years ago, and to date has not been held accountable."

"Stop right there," said Mayor Hasbrouck. "If my math is correct, Bill Perkins was not a member of our police force thirty years ago. Of what relevance is his prior service record to our community today?"

"A leopard does not change his spots, Mayor Hasbrouck," Turner replied succinctly. "The total character of a man should be known, especially that of the Chief of Police, as a matter of public record, for the safety, protection, trust and well-being of the city's residents."

"I agree with Mr. Turner," said Marco Tucci. "We should know as much as we can about our public officials, elected or appointed. And since it is the mayor's responsibility to appoint the police chief, and it's this council's job to confirm or deny the appointment, it is even more imperative that we have the full extent of him laid out for us."

"I, too, would like to hear what Mr. Turner has come to share with us," said Connors. "Although, I can assure you it will not have a bearing on the outcome of our own internal investigation hearing tomorrow. The merits of his behavior, past or present, will be treated separately."

I glanced at Paige to see what kind of reaction to this fiasco I could gauge from her facial expression and body language. Her thoughts were carefully hidden behind her copious notetaking.

Perkins may well survive tomorrow's hearing and still be removed from office as a result of the skewed portrait being painted of a youthful police officer brimming with hope and optimism, fictionally whitewashed to avoid addressing the real issues that existed in that hostile environment thirty years ago.

Hasbrouck acquiesced. "Please continue, Mr. Turner."

"Poughkeepsie, NY. July 1993. Bill Perkins was a rookie cop, out with his partner on his first real assignment: a back alley stabbing death of a decorated war veteran by three drug-fueled purported gang members. Rather than follow the evidence, Perkins formed a bond with the teens and decided to thwart the investigation by manufacturing a falsehood about his partner's reporting and tampering with crime scene evidence. As a result, the three teens were released from custody, enabling them to return to society to wreak more havoc."

"What proof do you have of these allegations, Mr. Turner?" inquired the councilwoman from the north ward.

He reached into his briefcase and held up a hardcover copy of *Dark Mercy* with its cover art showing a policeman in the shadows of an alleyway. "It's all documented here in this book," he answered.

"May we?" the councilwoman from the west ward asked, motioning him to pass the book around.

"This is a novel, a work of fiction," said the north ward woman upon examining the book. "It took place in a town called Fulton, New York. Is there such a place?"

"A veiled setting to protect the identity of the innocent victim and war hero who was murdered," Turner argued like the skilled lawyer he was.

Perkins leaned over and whispered something into the mayor's ear.

"Let it be entered into the record that the author of this novel is one Martin L. Turner, who I understand is a relative of the accusers? The mayor stared at Penrose intently for a vocal response to be recorded by the stenographer.

"Correct, Mayor. Martin is our father."

"And that the book bombed," I shouted from my seat, to the absolute delight of several council members.

Perkins smiled inwardly. So, I thought, did Paige.

"Strike that from the record, Margaret," the mayor directed the stenographer. "Mr. Cole, you will please refrain from any further outbursts, or you will be shown the door. Do I make myself clear?"

"Yes, your honor. Crystal." I didn't mind the mild rebuke from Hasbrouck. It was worth getting in a shot, even a fleeting one, to emphasize what a farce this proceeding was.

I watched as various members of the group nervously shifted in their seats, passed the book, and whispered remarks.

The mayor banged his gavel and called for order. "Ms. Turner, as the author of the exposé that brought William

Perkins' reputation under scrutiny, is there anything you'd care to add to your brother's recounting of the Poughkeepsie incident?"

Paige glanced at me before giving her answer. "Nothing, Mayor, other than a request to hear directly from Chief Perkins himself on the accusations brought against him before this august body. It has always been my desire to have Chief Perkins on the record."

I can attest to that. Since day one, that seemed to be the primary if not sole agenda item Paige Turner had pursued. And so, here we were, with this man's reputation on the line as he prepared to tell his side of the murky story. A story so laden with prejudice on both sides that the undiluted truth is impossible to discern anywhere, given the discriminatory lines still drawn in Everytown, USA. Looking at the composition of people in the room, the same governing body would never have existed in Poughkeepsie. The young Officer Perkins was savvy enough to understand that, and to take a stand on moral grounds. The same morals that could prove to be his undoing.

The mayor cleared his throat. "Chief Perkins, is there anything you would like to say in your defense, given the strong accusations alleged here today by the Turner family?"

Like a man facing a sentence for a crime he never meant to commit, at least not in the way it played out, and resigned to the consequences of his actions, Bill Perkins slowly rose to his feet.

"Council members. Associates. Friends. I stand before you accused of bending the law based only on my own interpretation of right and what is wrong. Of this I am guilty. I offer no excuse. For there is none that society would find acceptable. Was I wrong to take the law into my own hands? Yes. Was it improper for an officer of the law to interfere in an investigation that he was overseeing? Yes. Was it wrong for me to interject my personal feelings into a case involving three teens whose lives would be forever changed by this country's unequitable incarceration practices? Yes."

Bill Perkins leaned forward and placed his huge hands, knuckles down, on the table and stared at each council member in turn.

"But do I apologize? No. Spin it any way you like. I would still make the same decision today, in this town, if it involved your son or daughter or the children of any other citizen in this community in the same situation. To me, the law, applied without humanity, or exercised without mercy or forgiveness, is doomed to failure. Because laws are made by humans, and we humans are nothing if not imperfect creatures. Laws, too, are imperfect. Each of you must make your decision here. I live with the consequences of mine."

I had never heard Bill Perkins speak so eloquently. If he had been saving up his public statement for this time, in this venue, then I, for one, believe he made the right choice. Regardless of the outcome, Bill Perkins proved he was and always will be a man of his convictions. An imperfect man, like the rest of us, but a man willing to go out on that ledge for others.

He could have attacked any part of Penrose's accusations and won the day. These boys were not drugged-out criminals. And Johnny Wise was no hero. That's just storytelling. Bill Perkins decided not to tell his side of it. Instead, he chose to own up to it in a way the Turners would not or could not understand.

I tried to read the faces of the council members. By and large the males were stoic, the women appreciative to hear the truth from an honest man firsthand. No BS. No excuses. If Connors was unmoved, it was of little consequence.

Paige spoke up, permeating the silence. "Mr. Mayor, members of council, I would like to make a statement, for the record, if I may?"

"If it pleases the council, Ms. Turner would like to make a final statement for the record, after which we'll ask non-council participants to leave the room so the governing body can debate and take action. All those in favor of an additional statement from Ms. Turner, say 'aye.'"

The ayes carried the room. Penrose Turner scowled.

Paige Turner stood and addressed the room.

"Thank you, all. I wish to disengage myself from the accusations brought against Bill Perkins by the other members of the Turner family."

BAM! Penrose Turner fell back in his chair. Did Paige just switch sides again? The room was suddenly alive with chatter. To everyone's complete surprise, mine most of all, Paige Turner, in one swift stroke, threw her brother and father under the bus.

"Order, order," Mayor Hasbrouck shouted, banging his gavel repeatedly. "Will the officers kindly clear the room of all persons except members of council."

Connors left the room in a hurry, without a word to anyone. Penrose leapt to his feet and laid into his sister with a diatribe filled with expletives. He was about to slap her across the face for her apparent betrayal, but he never got the chance. I laid him out with a solid blow to the side of the head before two officers grabbed and pulled me out the door and carted me down the hall.

24

....

Sitting alone in the Frontier Airlines passenger lounge, it was like *déjà vu* all over again. To talk to, I had only Cliffy in his short-sleeved white shirt with the Frontier logo patch over the breast pocket. The seven-p.m. flight to Kansas City had just left. Paige was not on it. He confirmed that for me without any compensation this time. I guess he felt sorry for me.

He also confirmed a flight to Washington, D.C. had left at five-thirty p.m. with a passenger named Penrose M. Turner onboard. No doubt with a mouse over his left temple and his tail between his legs.

I hadn't seen Paige since I was dragged out of the city council meeting by two armed TPD officers. The cops had thrown me into their paddy wagon to cool me down until Chief Perkins came calling and bailed me out. Perkins confirmed the council had voted, four to one, not to sack him. He was now clear to await the hearing scheduled for the next day.

The cooling-down period effectively removed me from seeing Paige and her brother before they left city hall. Perkins told me brother and sister had left separately, but he didn't know the intended destination for either of them. He then thanked me for coming and supporting him. And for the left hook I landed on Penrose Turner's self-righteous head.

When I returned to the Marriott, I checked with the hotel clerk on duty. He advised that Ms. Turner had checked out of the hotel when she left in the morning but had come back after the city hall meeting to pick up her luggage, which she had left with the concierge. Then she left again around five p.m., destination unknown. I hustled to the airport and waited for about an hour, but she never showed.

Dejected, I walked slowly through the parking lot. The sun was just beginning to set over the Delaware. A peaceful time in the evening, to be sure, but an unsettling time for me. I felt like I needed closure with Paige after all we'd been through, yet I didn't necessarily want to shut the book on us just yet.

I spotted my car from a distance. It's hard to miss a 1966 metallic blue XKE in a near-vacant parking lot. Especially when the owner parks it diagonally and away from all other cars. But something was different. The top was down. I swore I'd left it up, as all day the sky had threatened rain. Then I saw the luggage piled in the rear seats. Two turquoise turtle-shell cases and a big purple striped Burberry bag. Paige Turner was stretched out in the passenger seat.

"My luggage wouldn't fit with the top up. So, I did what you showed me," she said flirtatiously.

"You did good, kid," I said, leaning down to kiss her passionately on the lips. "And you did *real* good this afternoon in front of city council. What an absolute stunner you pulled. I'm still in shock. Perkins is elated. How's Penrose taking it?"

"We're not on speaking terms. Again. His loss. Dad will know tonight."

"And us?"

"I forgive you."

"For what?"

"For doubting me, Mac. Admit it. You thought I went over to the opposition."

"I did."

"I told you all along. I just had to hear it from Perkins himself. That's all I ever wanted."

"I know."

"You clocked my brother. I don't think anyone has ever hit him – or stood up for me like that."

"Well, someone should have."

We drove back to the Marriott, brought her luggage up to Suite 3C, and ordered room service.

...

The next morning, we slept through breakfast and nearly missed lunch, for a different reason. By the time we got to police headquarters, the hearing was over. Shirley Mae's testimony and the letter from Penrose Turner sealed the deal for Connors' Internal Affairs panel. Perkins was completely absolved of any wrongdoing in connection with the data dump of the police records.

Connors, in turn, made a call to his contact at the FBI. Arrest warrants were issued for Martin and Penrose Turner for destruction of official documents, falsifying federal records and deceiving the public. Paige Turner's name was not included in the order.

At two p.m. while Paige chatted with Mary in the anteroom, both staring googly-eyed at the check we had received from the PBA for services rendered on the Perkins case, I had my session with Leroy Snyder, senior and junior together. Turns out, senior was just waiting for his son to come clean, and readily forgave him. Sometimes all a person wants is to hear the truth, straight from the horse's mouth.

The End

Printed in the United States
by Baker & Taylor Publisher Services